David
v.
GOD

MARY E. PEARSON

David
v.
GOD

HARCOURT, INC.

San Diego   New York   London

Library of Congress Cataloging-in-Publication Data
Pearson, Mary (Mary E.)
David v. God/by Mary E. Pearson.
p.   cm.
Summary: Certain that his death was a mistake, wise guy David James
finds himself teamed up with the "Queen of the Nerds" from his high school
in preparation for a debate with God.
[1. Near-death experiences—Fiction.   2. God—Fiction.   3. Heaven—Fiction.]
I. Title.   II. Title: David vs. God.   III. Title: David versus God.
PZ7.P32314Dav   2000
[Fic]—dc21   99-39421
ISBN 0-15-202058-6

Designed by Linda Lockowitz
The text was set in Dante.
First edition
H G F E D C B A
Printed in the United States of America

To Dennis,
with all my love

Contents

Acknowledgments

FOR SOMEONE who lives and breathes words on a daily basis, I am feeling quite inadequate now as I try to express my gratitude to those who have made this book possible.

First, thank you to my mom and dad, Helen and Odell Stark, who always knew the value of books, and even when money was nonexistent somehow made sure there were books on our shelves. I am also grateful to Dorothy and Cecil Pearson, who never blinked an eye when I said I was writing a book and who eagerly devoured my first manuscript.

Special thanks to Judith Enderle for her invaluable

advice, encouragement, and hand-holding. She went above and beyond the call of duty.

I never could have made it to the finish line without my on-line writing buddies, Donna Figurski, Kim Williams-Justesen, Jill Rubalcaba, Roberta Updegraff, and Karen Romano Young. They always had the right word at the right time to keep me going. Mucho thanks to you guys.

Enormous thanks to my editor, Karen Grove, who has been so supportive. She has put up with my incessant newbie questions—with a smile—and provided gentle, expert guidance through the whole process. Her enthusiasm for this book meant the world to me.

My deepest gratitude to my family, who always believed and put up with my vacant stares as "story" took over. Thanks to my daughters, Karen and Jessica, for their expert, on-the-spot consultations, and to my husband, Dennis, my inspiration.

And of course my ultimate thanks to the Big Kahuna, who makes every journey an adventure.

David
V.
GOD

1
Wrong Turn?

"OH, MAN!"

David had thought he might be dying as he looked past his chest and saw his intestines splayed out before him, but when his viewpoint changed—when he was no longer looking across at the carnage, but looking down on it—that was when he started to get worried. He hovered over his body like a police helicopter surveying a crime scene.

"Oh, God! I'm doing that floating thing. This isn't good." David clawed at the air, trying to get back to his body, but he felt himself getting sucked up higher and higher.

"Cool, huh, David?"

David looked up. Things were going from bad to

worse. There was Booger. Blond dreadlocks and all. No way was David going to spend all of eternity with him! He clawed more frantically.

"I don't think it's going to do any good, David."

He looked up again. It was Mrs. Dunne, his biology teacher. In fact, everyone who had been in the van with him was floating like a bunch of parachuters, except they were falling up, not down. Natalie. Jason. Ernesto. Marie. They were all goofoffs who had gotten stuck in Mrs. Dunne's van for the field trip. Except for Marie. She wasn't a goof-off, but she came late to school that day and the other cars and vans were already full. She had to take the only empty seat left, which happened to be in the van with the goof-offs. Not that they were dumb or anything. For God's sake, it was Honors Bio. But even smart kids could have attitudes.

David knew this probably wasn't the time or place, but he couldn't pass up the opportunity. He never could. In those few seconds after they had crashed through the guardrail and their van became airborne—even then the words had flashed through his head, but he hadn't had a chance to say them.

Now he looked across at his teacher—her body

being sucked up like his—and asked, "Make a wrong turn, Mrs. Dunne?"

That was all it took for the diarrhea of comments to begin.

"Hey, Mrs. Dunne, does this mean we get an extra day to turn our homework in?" Jason sputtered.

"I don't think I filled out the form for *this* field trip," Natalie added.

"Do we get extra credit for this?" Booger asked.

Ernesto chimed in with his Hispanic drawl, "Hey, Mrs. Dunne, from now on, can I always ride with *you* on field trips?"

"No way!" David said. "When word gets out about the Viper ride, there's gonna be a waiting list to get in her car!"

"Are you all crazy?" Marie interrupted, her anger a stark contrast to their warped humor. "Don't you get it? We're dead! *D-E-A-D. Dead!*"

"Hey, lighten up, Marie," Jason said, but her words had already jerked David back to reality.

He wasn't in sixth period waiting for the bell to ring. He was—

"Not me!" David snapped. "Maybe you, but I'm

not dead! No way!" He looked back down at his body, which had become a small, indistinguishable speck. He had to get back. He clawed and kicked, but with a last great *whoosh,* he was sucked out of sight of the speck that had been his life. His last words echoed throughout the heavens: "Hey, you can't do this! My dad's a lawyer..."

2

A Little Drool Goes a Long Way

DAVID SAT in the back of the bus. He didn't know how he had gotten there. It didn't make any sense, but he guessed heaven didn't have to make sense.... *That is, if I am in heaven,* he thought. But it was all white and glowy, even the bus, like he imagined heaven would be. Yeah, he was in heaven all right. He looked at his fellow travelers, the same six from the van. They all just sat there contentedly, looking out the windows at scenery that wasn't there. Even Natalie, with her purple spiked hair, sat there tapping her foot like she was on her way to a Deadhead concert. It was too weird. Only Marie, sitting straight in her prim navy blue cardigan, seemed the slightest bit agitated as she dug her fingers into the seat in front of her.

David looked farther down the aisle. There was Mrs. Dunne way up in the front seat—thank God she wasn't driving. This was crazy! Why was he sitting here when this bus needed to make a *big* U-turn, like right now. He started to stand up, but immediately the bus driver's eyes were on him and he pointed to a sign posted at the front of the bus.

ALL PASSENGERS MUST REMAIN

SEATED WHILE BUS IS IN MOTION

David started to sit obediently back down, but then caught himself. *What's he going to do? Kill me?* He marched up the aisle and stopped beside the driver, a tall middle-aged fellow with thinning hair— no wings.

"There's been a mistake," David said. "I'm not supposed to be here. Not yet. You've got to take me back."

"Me, too!" Marie jumped up from her seat and rushed to join David at the front of the bus. "I don't think I belong here, either. Not yet, anyway."

The bus driver rolled his eyes. His head—his whole body—seemed to wriggle with annoyance.

"Just sit down and enjoy the scenery. God doesn't make mistakes."

"What scenery? All I see is a freakin' white fog bank out there!" David yelled.

"Me, too," Marie meekly added.

The bus driver raised one eyebrow. "Only white fog?"

David and Marie nodded.

"Here, hold this." The bus driver shoved the loose steering wheel into David's hands and whipped out a beat-up spiral notebook. "Let's see," he said as he ran his finger down the page. "Dinner with Mona. Haircut. Lube job. David...David... Yup! Here you are! David Jones. March thirteenth. Dead."

"Jones! You idiot! My last name is *James*. David *James!*"

"Could you check my name, too? Marie Smythe. Smythe with a *y*."

The driver snapped the book shut. "No need to check. Mistake there, too!" He shrugged his shoulders and smiled like he had forgotten to put the cheese on a cheeseburger. He started to take the steering wheel back, but David angrily held it out of his reach.

"That's it? What are you going to do about—"

"Hey, David, check it out!" Jason called from the middle of the bus. The whole group, even Mrs. Dunne, was crowded around two windows. "The waves are awesome!"

"Yyyow!" Booger wailed, and then the whole group laughed, exchanging high fives and nods of approval.

David turned back to the driver. "What about them? Check their names."

The driver shook his head. "No mistakes there. It's rather obvious that they see more than white fog."

David didn't know how this heaven stuff worked, but he was certain he was being taken farther and farther away from his body—a little "incidental" that he would need to return to his old life—and this wannabe angel didn't seem to be the least bit concerned about his "little" mistake. David decided to try a line he had heard his mom and dad use countless times.

"Who's your supervisor? I want to talk to him," he said.

The driver's cheeks bulged, and little puffs of air escaped through his lips as he tried to suppress his amusement. "Did you hear that, Sam? He wants to talk to my *supervisor.*" He doubled over with a bellowing laugh and tears streamed down his cheeks.

Sam? David looked around the bus, but there was no Sam. *Great,* he thought, *this angel is not only incompetent but also delusional.*

The driver straightened up and returned to his serious demeanor. "My supervisor is God...and let's see...you want to *talk* to him." He whipped out the spiral notebook once again and began running his finger down the pages. "Talk...talk...Nope! Lots of close calls. Plenty of notes here about you always yammering his name, but no record here of you *talking* to God—at least not in the last decade or so."

David felt his face start to tighten up the way his father's did when he was losing his patience. "I'm not talking about in the past, *sir.* I'm talking about now. I want to talk to God—*now!*"

"Oh no—it doesn't work that way. If you didn't talk to him down there, you can't talk to him up here. A little rule we have." The driver smiled politely and then added, "But how about wrestling?"

"*What?*"

"Wrestling," the driver repeated. "You know, on a

mat. Pinning. God loves a good wrestling match. Do you wrestle?"

David's eyes grew wide and blank. Conversations here seemed to take unexpected turns. He was afraid to get pulled into this twisted logic, but he was also afraid not to—his body was getting farther and farther away.

"No. I don't wrestle," he answered.

"Archery?" the driver suggested.

"No."

"Track? A little fifty-yard dash with God?"

"No."

The driver raised one eyebrow, visibly annoyed. "Football? Tennis? Five-card draw?"

David shook his head. "No."

"Well, just what *do* you do?" the driver asked.

David fidgeted. *God!* This was just like the conversation in the principal's office. He had pulled some awesome pranks over the years—stories he and his friends would rehash on Friday nights—but none could compare with the prank that had warranted *both* of his parents' leaving work and coming to the principal's office. It had been his best effort yet, because he'd had a captive audience of two thousand students and teachers. And the beauty of it all was that it had been completely spontaneous. He hadn't even planned it. It was just this little gem begging him to take advantage. He did.

He remembered he was late to school that day and was waiting in the attendance office for a back-to-class pass. Mrs. Graves, the principal, was just finishing the day's announcements in the little room that held the intercom system. The secretary handed his pass to him and walked away at the same time the principal left the tiny room, which was adjacent to the office. David was alone and could see the microphone sitting on the table.

The next thing he knew he was inside the little room making announcements of his own. He had locked the door behind him and, in spite of the banging and yelling on the other side, David proceeded to do his own stand-up routine for the whole school. He outdid Seinfeld. He then moved on to gossip, who was bonking who, and finally negotiated his own exit from his command station.

He had to admit that by then he was pretty scared. There was a small window in the room and he had witnessed the progression of colors and expressions that moved over the principal's face as David entertained the school. But it was his moment of glory. This little stunt would forever earn him an honored place in the Halls of Balls.

Two hours later, when his mom and dad showed up, David waited for his father to start defending him—right or wrong—the way he defended his clients. After all, David was his son. But it didn't work out that way. As Mrs. Graves retold every detail, David watched those already familiar colors and expressions pass over his father's face. He wasn't his father's client. He was a dead man. Mrs. Graves had an ally.

David had been smart enough to circumvent suspension. It had been a condition of his exit. But when you're on the verge of hyperventilating, it's hard to think of everything. He knew Mrs. Graves would not go back on her word about the suspension, but he also knew she was not one to be outdone.

In a calm, calculating voice that rivaled even his father's best courtroom performance, she began to weave her web. "Perhaps, Mr. and Mrs. James, David just needs more outlets for his—*creative energies.*" Mrs. Graves turned to David. "Are you involved in any after-school sports, David? Football? Track?"

"No."

"Tennis?"

"No."

"I see. Any clubs? French Club? Chess Club?"

"No."

"Hmm. Band?"

Oh, she was good. "No. I'm not involved in anything."

David grimaced as his mother walked right into the trap. "Mrs. Graves, is there something you could suggest?"

Mrs. Graves opened a thin pamphlet on her desk and began running her finger down the pages. "Let's see . . . Crestview High has something for everybody. I'm sure we can find something that will channel your energies more positively, David," she said.

"Mrs. Graves, I really don't need—"

"Oh! Here we go. This would be perfect for you, David." She raised her eyes to look squarely into David's and smiled. David felt his knees get rubbery even though he wasn't standing. Mrs. Graves could do that.

"The Speech and Debate Club. How perfectly apropos, considering your bent for public speaking. They meet three days a week after school."

No way, David thought. *The Speech and Debate*

Club is for losers. It is the land of the dweebs. Only nerds join. No way will I—

"He'll be there, Mrs. Graves," his father said.

And that was that. There was no discussion. No more negotiating. David was whisked onto the Speech and Debate roster faster than he had slipped into the tiny room with the microphone. Mrs. Graves had her prey wrapped up as tightly as a moth in the clutches of a black widow.

"Debate," David said.

"What?" the confused driver asked.

"Debate. You asked what I do. I debate. I'll debate God," David said.

"Oh, I don't know. That sounds a whole lot like talking to me, and I already told you about that."

"No. It's not the same thing at all." David remembered what Mr. Ferguson, the speech advisor, had told him at his first club meeting. He repeated it for the driver. "It's the same difference as between a well-aimed spitwad and drool. One just sort of dribbles out your mouth, the other is sure to get someone's attention." David took a deep breath and went on. "It's an art, that's what it is. There's a whole club for debate and everything. And I'm in it—the president, in fact...Yeah, if I can't talk to

God, I'll debate him. I've got to go back. I want to debate God." David felt like he had just drooled all over his shirt.

"Debate, huh?" The driver looked David up and down. "I'll check on it and let you know. Have a seat."

As they returned to their seats Marie elbowed David and whispered, "The president?"

"*Shhh!*" David whispered back. Only Marie would know he had lied. She was the Nerdess Supreme. Queen of the Losers. Her Royal Dweeb. The *real* president of the Speech and Debate Club.

3

Could Things Be Worse?

DAVID SAT ALONE in the back of the bus watching Natalie pick a wedge. He guessed some things never changed, even up in heaven.

It had all happened so fast, it was just now starting to sink in. They were dead. All of them, at least temporarily. He and Marie might be going back, but the others... some heavenly insight told David that their feet were already firmly planted in the clouds. They were already reaching out, exploring eternity through the scenery that passed by the bus windows.

He looked over at Jason. Jason was his best friend. Jock Extraordinaire. David had enjoyed the fringe benefits of having a chick magnet for a best friend. At parties, when girls swarmed around Jason, he could always count on a few wayward bees buzzing his way. Not that David was chopped meat or anything, but Jason had a way with girls. Smooth. He knew all the moves. The nod of the head, the smile, the sideways glance that made every girl think she was the one.

Jason was always willing to help David carry out his wild ideas, too. Like the night they took every piece of furniture from the teachers' patio and put it up on top of the roof for all to see the next day—complete with marginally dressed dummies representing their "favorite" teachers. Or the time they streaked across the football field during a spirit assembly, wearing only their boxers and nylon stockings over their heads. David smiled as he thought about Jason's nervous hiccuping laugh when Mrs. Graves questioned them about the incident. But she never could pin it on them—the stockings had done their job.

David's smile faded. Were those times all over?

Now Jason was sitting there talking to Booger like they were about to collaborate on brain surgery. Booger! Booger didn't even qualify as a goof-off because it was too natural for him—it was still a mystery to David how he ever got into Honors Bio.

Ernesto sat there listening to them both, nodding his head in that too-cool way he always did. Nothing could fluster Ernesto. Not heaven. Not even Mrs. Graves. And his humor was so dry it could even make David choke. He could spit out line after line without ever cracking a smile. You had to be fast around Ernesto or you'd end up being the butt—like Booger had been countless times, and never even knew it.

Natalie continued to pick at her wedge and though it provided the perfect opportunity for David to break up the monotomy of the bus ride, he didn't jump on this one. Somehow the self-appointed president of the dweebs just wasn't feeling witty right now.

The bus pulled to a stop and the driver stood up, laying the steering wheel on his seat. "This is it, folks. Watch your step getting out. You don't want to slip and end up *who knows where.*"

David could see the driver was amused with his heavenly humor. It made David sick. Whenever teachers—or wannabe angels—tried to be funny they just ended up looking stupid. He and Marie shuffled behind the others.

"What about us? Should we get out here, too?" David asked.

The driver whispered over his shoulder, "What do ya think, Sam? Should the kid and his girlfriend get out here?"

"Oh, wait a minute," David said. "You've got that wrong. She's not my—"

"Yes," the driver said. "Sam says to exit here and wait until you hear if the debate has been approved."

David looked around. "Who the hell is Sam?" he asked.

The driver's cheeks bulged once more, but he only rolled his eyes and shook his head as he led the group down a long sidewalk that led to a small white doorway. Marie whispered to David, "You better watch your language. Remember where you are! *He* might be listening."

"I'm not worried," David said as he wiped away a line of sweat that was just forming over his lip. "But I'll tell you what scares me, is when someone mistakes *you* for my girlfriend. Now, that's scary."

"No, that's just your fantasy. Dream on," Marie said, and walked ahead.

As they made their way down the sidewalk, Mrs. Dunne held back until David caught up with her. She put a chubby arm around David's shoulders and said, "Now, David, I don't want you to worry about a thing. I know that little incident with the guardrail was unexpected, but things could have turned out worse, and—"

David was incredulous. His frustration finally boiled over.

"How, Mrs. Dunne? How could things have possibly turned out any worse?" He then proceeded to answer his own question. "Let's see. I suppose we could have actually made it to our destination and had to sit through one of your miserable, boring lessons. Yeah, that would have been worse. Or maybe after crashing, nothing at all would have happened, and instead of zipping up here to heaven we could have all just become fertilizer—like *you* always taught us in biology. Or maybe you could have died in that freakin' orange dress you wear every Tuesday, and you would have to spend the rest of eternity in that thing!"

Mrs. Dunne's arm dropped from David's shoulders and her face began to scrunch up. She looked like one of those withered apple dolls his mother had once bought at a craft fair. *Oh, God!* She was going to cry. David could handle barbs from Marie's mouth, but tears from an old lady—they were more than his match. He began to dance around her with his hands up, trying to stem the flow.

"Mrs. Dunne, I didn't mean it. Really. I was joking. Okay?" The scrunching reached a peak and David pleaded more earnestly, "Please, Mrs. Dunne, don't—"

It was not a pretty sight. He found that watching an old lady cry was not unlike holding his brother's head up over the toilet as he puked. Kind of made you want to do it, too.

"Way to go, pinhead," Natalie said to David as she put her arm around the sobbing Mrs. Dunne.

He watched as Natalie led her away to the front of the group, leaving him alone to walk behind the others. When did Natalie, with all her purple spikes and chains, get so softhearted? But her words still rang in his ears. *Way to go, pinhead.*

He felt like a pinhead. No, worse than that. Lower. Like gum on the bottom of a shoe. Except for the little guardrail incident, Mrs. Dunne had always been a good teacher. Better than most, actually, and she had always taken the goof-offs, especially him, in stride.

He didn't know now whether to keep his big mouth shut or go for some conciliatory comment, but flapping his mouth came more naturally, so he said, "Hey, Mrs. Dunne, my mom has an orange dress, too. She says it may make her look like a pumpkin, but it makes her feel cheerful. Hey, Mrs. Dunne ... wait up ..."

4
The Answer Is...

WHEN THE DRIVER pulled open the ordinary white door at the end of the sidewalk, David expected to see an ordinary white room behind it, but the scene that was revealed was anything but ordinary.

Only Booger was able to express the feelings of the whole group. "Whooh! Rad!" he said as he walked through the doorway. The rest stood huddled together, mouths open, gawking.

"Toto, I don't think we're in Kansas anymore," Natalie finally mumbled.

They had never seen anything like it. They were at the entrance to a train station that appeared to go on for miles in either direction. It made Penn Station look like Petticoat Junction. The spires reached so high they got lost in a soft mist. Leaded windows in the distant ceilings fractured beams of light onto the hurried travelers below. David was amazed. There were hundreds—no, *thousands*—of travelers hurrying to get on and off trains, their excited chatter creating a pleasant roar.

David stepped near the driver. He was puzzled. "I'm not saying I'm not impressed or anything, but why do you need a train station up in heaven? I mean, can't you just zap yourself where you want to go?"

The driver looked equally puzzled. "Well, yes, I suppose we could. But why would we want to? Getting there is half the fun. You should see our airport."

David didn't have time to ponder the explanation. The driver hurried to the front of the group and said, "Stay together now. I'm taking you to the Waiting Room for your orientation, then you will be free to explore heaven!"

They followed behind the driver like enchanted little children on their first trip to Disneyland. This wasn't just a train station—a place to take you away to somewhere else. It was a place to *be* as well. Musicians, vendors, and street entertainers of every sort dotted the cavern.

They passed a mime who had a small crowd gathered around him. He appeared to be confined in an imaginary box that was rapidly growing smaller. His hands searched along the box's walls for an escape, and then suddenly his eyes caught David's. He shook his head sadly from side to side and then wiped away an imaginary tear.

"I think he wants you to help him, David," Natalie said.

David shivered. The guy gave him the creeps. "Oh, darn, I think I left my imaginary keys at home. I guess he's gonna have to help himself. C'mon, let's go." David pushed ahead of Natalie to walk at the front of the group. He found himself next to Marie, who seemed to be taking everything in systematically. Not enjoying it, just observing, classifying for future reference. That was creepy, too—she was like a machine. Why did she have to end up with their group? She didn't fit in.

"Stay together now," the driver urged. "We're almost there. We'll be turning right at that hallway up ahead."

David was relieved. Maybe now this whole mess would get cleared up.

Just before they turned down the hallway, they encountered a group of smelly, strangely dressed people. They all had long tangled hair, with colorful headbands tied across their foreheads. One of them, with a fringed, beaded vest, strummed a sadly out-of-tune guitar—but it didn't really matter—his strained voice nearly drowned out the guitar's warped melody. David and Jason looked at each other with raised eyebrows. Jason leaned close to David and whispered, "Ya think these are the 'heavenly hosts'?"

"You moron!" Natalie snapped in a hushed voice. "They're not angels! They're *hippies*."

David noticed that Natalie said "hippies" like she was uttering the most sacred of all words. He didn't know what the big deal was. He had seen pictures of his dad with long hair and a beard and figured he must have been a hippie, too. Still, it was strange to see the real thing face-to-face, especially up here in heaven, where he'd thought everyone would look the same and they would all wear long white robes. These hippies were definitely "unique."

One of them stepped into David's path. "Peace,

brother!" he proclaimed as he held up his hand with two fingers pointed in a **V**. David looked at Jason and shrugged. He didn't have a clue how this bro handshake worked. Finally David held up his hand in a similar manner and tapped his fingers against the hippie's poised hand. "Yeah," David said, "same to you, buddy." The hippie shrugged his shoulders and returned to his group.

"Let's move along now," the driver urged, and David gladly heeded his words.

The orientation took place in a small, plain room down the hallway adjacent to the station. David slouched down in a hard, folding chair next to Jason as the driver went through his spiel. Heaven was not at all what David had envisioned. Ernesto sat in front of him, and David kept looking at Ernesto's back, expecting wings to sprout at any moment. The driver droned on, but David didn't hear too much. He tuned him out the same way he did his teachers. He wasn't planning on staying, so what was the point?

"...and in the near-distant future," the driver went on, "each of you will have your own personal appointment with God—but you don't need to worry about sticking around. We'll summon you wherever you are. It is advisable to stay together in your group, at least for the first few days, until you get your bearings. The brochures on the table suggest some key spots to visit. Other than that, there are no rules for you to remember. Oh, and there is a Coke machine down the hall to your right and a coffee bar a little past that. And the answer, David, is yes."

David was caught off-guard by the mention of his name. "Excuse me—what?"

"The answer is yes," the driver repeated.

David wondered if this wingless angel–Alex Trebek wannabe was getting on anybody else's nerves. All of his answers led nowhere. "Is this *Jeopardy* or something," David asked, "and I am supposed to come up with the question?"

The driver echoed David's annoyance by wriggling his whole body like he had on the bus. "You asked if you could debate God," he said slowly. "The answer is yes. Look out the window." He motioned to a window that looked out on the station. David walked over and pulled aside the vertical blinds that covered it.

There was only one word that could express

David's feelings right now, but he thought about Marie's warning: *Remember where you are.* Instead he concentrated on keeping his stomach out of his throat. There on the huge station marquee, which normally announced the arrivals and departures of trains, was a new announcement:

THE GREAT DEBATE!

DAVID V. GOD

9:00 A.M. TOMORROW. EVERYONE WELCOME!

David reached for the nearest chair and slid numbly into it. He was screwed! No—worse than that. He was dead—no, he was that already. He was something, and he couldn't even think of a word for it! Oh, he'd make a great debater. David went back to his first thought. He was screwed!

Booger laughed. "Hey, David, do you see that? Your name's up there. Cool."

"Yeah, I see it, Booger," David answered.

"Of course, you will have to do all the talking, David, since you're the one who challenged God," the driver said, "but Marie is on your team, too, and she can help you prepare."

"Oh, that makes me feel so much better," David

said as he closed his eyes and ran his fingers through his hair.

"I'll give you this, David," Ernesto said. "You got balls."

"Hey, bro, forget about this debate thing," Jason said as he pulled a chair up next to David's at the table. "There's too many cool things up here to check out. Why would you want to go back? Remember, no rules. That means no homework. Look at this, David." Jason shoved a brochure in David's face.

The whole group, except Marie, pulled chairs up to the table and excitedly began poring over the brochures. David opened the colorful pamphlet, but he couldn't share Jason's excitement. He let the paper slip from his hand to the floor. No one noticed except Marie. She grabbed his hand and pulled him to a corner of the room, lowering her voice so the others wouldn't hear.

"They're dead, David. Dead as doornails. They're supposed to be here. But we're not. I'm sure of it. We've got to send them on their way so we can prepare for this debate. We don't have much time."

David stared at Marie. She was serious. He couldn't believe it. "C'mon, Marie! Me debate God while every freakin' angel in heaven watches? I don't know why I ever suggested it! It was stupid. What chance do I have against *God*?"

"You won't have any chance at all, David—if you don't even try. Please. I *have* to go back. I have my reasons."

Jeez! That's just like Marie, David thought. She was so serious—so organized about everything. She probably already had all of her reasons outlined, cataloged, and filed. David couldn't think of a single reason why he *had* to go back. Just that he wanted to.

"Hey, David! Look at this!" Jason called. "It's the tallest roller coaster in the universe! C'mon, bro, let's go."

David watched the others push their chairs back, eager to go find the celestial ride. The group shuffled out, but Jason stopped at the door and looked back at David, waiting. "Bro?" he called again. Jason expected him to go, too.

And why shouldn't I? David thought. *We're best friends and do everything together. Why shouldn't I just go?* David took in a deep breath and let it shudder back out across his lips. Hanging with Jason and taking a spin on a wild roller coaster sounded like a lot more fun than preparing for a debate. He looked at Marie. Her eyes were still fixed on him.

"You go ahead, Jason." David sighed. "Maybe I'll catch up with you later. Me and Marie...we have some talking to do."

5

Risky Business

THE MORE DAVID thought about it, the more he liked the idea. That little stunt in the intercom room was peanuts compared to this. *David versus God.* Scary, but exciting. And he had The Brain on his team. Marie could do all the work. She was a robot—an automaton. She'd come up with the main arguments, and he could polish them to perfection. Yeah, together they could—

"Hello, anybody home?" Marie interrupted his daydreaming. "The others are gone, David. We've got to get busy. I wonder if there's any paper around here so we can jot down some notes." She walked over to the table and shuffled through the scattered brochures. "No blank paper here."

"What's the matter?" David joked. "Is your hard drive so overloaded that you can't remember everything we say?"

David waited for even the thinnest smile from Marie.

"It would be my RAM, David," she corrected, "assuming I were a computer, which I'm not. Now, are you going to help me or are you going to live up to your reputation and flake?"

Whooh, the ice queen, David thought. No hint of a smile there. Just a few minutes earlier, David had thought there might be a babe behind the robot. When she had grabbed his hand and pulled him across the room, for the briefest moment he thought he had seen the girl that Marie was. Not bad looking, despite the dweeby clothes. Better than some he had dated. Maybe she just needed to loosen up a little. But now he could see that she was microchip through and through—and computers don't loosen up.

"Okay, C-3PO, let's go look for some paper," he said.

They both walked toward the door, but before they reached it, the door swung open with a loud bang and the driver entered. His eyes barely showed over the stacks of paper and books and assorted boxes he carried in his arms. He staggered toward the table and let his load spill onto it.

"What's this?" David asked.

"You need paper, don't you?" the driver said. "And I brought some other things you might need. A dictionary. Thesaurus. Farmer's almanac. Pencils. Erasers. Lots of erasers."

"Farmer's almanac?" Marie questioned.

"You never know," the driver answered matter-of-factly. "Oh, and God sent over some of his journals, too. He thought you might find them helpful." The driver lifted a few from the pile and read their spines. "Let's see, we have Romans...Revelation—that one will get your eyes spinning—and we have Isaiah—oh, here we go. Genesis. He said you should probably read this one first. You might find some helpful tidbits in it."

"Tidbits? Yeah, right," David said. He took the journal from the driver's hand. "Like God's going to try to help us win. I don't think so. We'll just stick to our own strategies." He threw the journal back onto the table.

"Suit yourself." The driver shrugged and turned to leave the room.

"Hey, thanks for the paper, though," David called after him, trying to soften his last words; after all, the wingless angel seemed to carry some weight around here. "Uh—sir—do you have a name or beeper number or something in case we have to get hold of you again?"

The driver turned around, seemingly pleased that David had taken a personal interest in him. "No beeper numbers up here, thanks to Sam, but I do have a name. Leonardo. But my friends call me—"

"Nardo?" David offered. He couldn't help it. His mouth was faster than his brain.

The driver turned his head from side to side, furrowed his brow, and then smiled. "Leo, actually, but Nardo has a nice ring, too. It'll do." He opened the door and left.

David couldn't help but laugh, even if Marie wasn't amused. "Ya know, I think old Nardo's starting to grow on me," he said.

"Yes, well, don't get too attached," Marie said as she started straightening the disorderly supplies into neat piles. "I don't plan on staying here too long. Let's get to work."

David watched her methodical movements. She

never strayed from her goal. It disgusted him. "Jeez! Don't you *ever* lighten up? Why do you take everything so seriously?"

Marie paused, raising her dark brown eyes to pierce David's. "Let's turn that around for a minute, *Mr. James*. Why is everything a joke to you? Don't *you* ever take anything seriously?"

"I asked you first," David said, hearing the whine in his own voice. He silently shuddered at the ground he had just lost.

"But *my* question was more important," Marie said without wavering, and then she curled the corners of her mouth into a forced, tight-lipped smile.

That did it. David imagined a hundred ways to wipe that smirk off her face. He wondered what the penalty was in heaven for killing someone who was already dead. She was the Hard Drive from Hell, the Evil Master Cylinder, the—

"Well, David? No answer?" she taunted.

—the putty in his hands. He still had a card up his sleeve. It was only to be used in extreme cases. In fact, he had never used it. It was risky. Big-time risky. But David was a risk taker, no question about that. He'd try what Jason called "revealing your feminine side." Jason had read about it in a magazine. He said it worked like a charm. Earned megapoints. Girls ate it up.

David wasn't sure it would work on a computer chip, but he'd give it a try. What did he have to lose? He knew exactly why he was a goof-off. He'd spill his guts and watch her melt.

"Ya wanna know, Marie? Okay, I'll tell you. Sit down."

They pulled up chairs opposite each other at the table. David could feel his heart pounding. Step one was accomplished, but from here he wasn't exactly sure where to go. "I have my reasons for being what you call a goof-off, but I'm not sure you'd understand."

"I'm listening," Marie said.

David squirmed. This "revealing stuff" was more uncomfortable than he expected. He ran his fingers through his hair and continued, "I don't think of it as being a goof-off like you do. Just more realistic. That's all."

Marie's penetrating gaze disappeared as David reflected on the events that had altered the course of his personality. "I used to be more goal oriented than I am now, but then some things happened that opened my eyes." He took a deep breath. Did he really want to do this? Marie sat silently, waiting. He had no choice. "When I was a freshman I tried out for the West City Baseball League. It's the league everyone wants to be in, and there was no question I'd make it. I had pitched our team to the playoffs in the Junior League the year before. My parents had invested in hours and hours of private coaching. I was good. Better than good. The best. I was going to be the next Nolan Ryan. Well, tryouts came, and I made the team all right, but not as the pitcher. In fact, I wasn't given a real position at all. Just an alternate. The sponsor's son made pitcher. My dad raised a stink, but it didn't do any good. All of my work— all the hours, *years,* of practicing—were for nothing...nothing. I was suddenly a nobody because someone played the game better than I did—and I'm not talking about the game of baseball."

David took another deep breath. He felt like he was standing naked in front of Marie. Jason hadn't told him that exposing himself would be painful. He wove his fingers together and went on. "But that wasn't all. About that same time something else happened. You remember, a few years ago, the city treasurer who embezzled all that money from the city?"

"Yes," Marie answered.

"Well, did you ever notice on the evening news who was defending him?" David asked.

"No, not really."

"It was my dad. The guy was as guilty as sin and everyone knew it. My dad knew it. When I asked him why he was defending a guy he knew was guilty, he said it wasn't a question of right or wrong, but a question of strategy and making the right moves. You see, I had always thought of my dad as the Defender of Justice, but he was just one of the game players, too. I realized then that you can't take anything too seriously, because nothing is really how it appears. It's all just a big game ... only a game."

David felt empty. He was no longer concerned with how his words were affecting Marie, but with how they affected him. Spoken aloud, his thoughts took on a chilling new reality.

He looked up. Marie's eyes were intently on him. Maybe she did understand. Maybe she was melting.

"That's it?" Marie said as she laughed. "One little bump in the road and you give up? You screw up your whole life because you didn't get to be star pitcher ... and you don't like the way your dad earns the piles of money that put the designer clothes on your back? Oh, David, you poor thing."

Her last stab was the worst.

He felt the knife twisting in his gut.

"Go to hell, Marie!" David yelled. He slammed his chair back against the wall and headed for the door. He'd get Jason for this. Here he had bared his soul, and she had promptly filleted it. It was his own fault. He never should have tried Jason's strategy. It was only meant for beings of the human persuasion. He pulled open the door.

"David!" Marie called. "Wait. I'm sorry. Please." Her voice became a soft whisper. "Please give me a chance to explain."

David paused at the open door, his back still to Marie. This was probably a big mistake, but no one ever accused David of not taking risks. He closed the door and turned around.

"I'm listening," he said coldly.

David scrutinized Marie, but as he watched, he began to feel his anger subside. She was changing before his eyes. He saw the color drain from her face. Her cheek twitched, and she looked down into her fidgeting hands as if the words she searched for were there.

David walked back to his chair and sat down. "Go ahead," he said.

Marie's eyes remained fixed on her hands as she talked. "I know what I'm like, David. I'm not stupid, and I'm not deaf. I hear the comments, the snickers...the names. Microchip Marie. The Byte Bitch. 'Don't stand too close to her, you might get frostbite.' Queen of the Nerds."

David shifted uncomfortably in his seat. The last one had been his personal favorite.

"But I have my reasons, too, for being the way I am. You call it cold, unsocial, nerdy. Probably a lot of other things I haven't even thought of. But I call it focused. I have to be focused, David."

"Why, Marie? Why can't you relax and kick back just once? Would it kill you?" David asked.

"It's hard for you to understand, but not every kid at Crestview High lives in a huge house with sprawling green lawns. We don't all have housekeepers, gardeners, and private tutors. Some of us don't have DJs at our birthday parties, and we certainly don't get cars, complete with phones, as presents. Don't get me wrong, I'm not complaining, but you asked me why I'm so serious and I have to show you the whole picture."

David nodded and slid lower in his chair. She had described his life to a *T*.

Marie continued. "The flip side of all that is public assistance, public transportation, and a lunch card that tells everyone that the government is paying your way—"

"Okay, your life has been tough, Marie," David interrupted, "but what does that have to do with you being so serious?"

"The only way I'll ever see college is through a scholarship. I *have* to be the best. I can't ever let up. I have to do this for my mom. She was a good student, but she missed her chance to go to college because she lost her focus."

"What do you mean?"

"She put her college plans on hold so she could put her husband through school. Once he had his degree he said 'Thank you very much' and left, and she never saw him again. By then she already had me, and the twins were on the way. No chance of going back to college then. She never complains, but she works two jobs just to keep a roof over our heads and food on the table. She used to be a pretty woman, but now she just looks tired."

"Can't you get a job and help her out?"

"She won't let me. She says nothing can stand in the way of my grades. So that's why I work so hard. My goal isn't a car or designer clothes. I just want to get into college so I can get a good job and support my mom, maybe even send her back to school. And I can't let anyone or *anything* keep me from that—even being dead. That's why I've got to go back."

Marie took a deep breath, and added, "I'm sorry that when you told me about your life I was so..."

"Callous?" David offered.

"Yes," Marie said, looking back down at her lap. "You see, I've never been very good at that sort of thing. My focus has always been goals, not feelings, but I really do know that I'm not the only one with problems...I'm sorry."

"Hey, forget it," David said. "It was worth it just to see that layer of ice on you melt for a few minutes—and I'm sorry about what I said, too—ya know, the 'go to hell' thing. I guess that was sort of a stupid thing to say, considering where we are and all."

"I deserved it," Marie said.

"No, you deserved something more creative than that."

"Yeah, I guess I did," she agreed.

David stared at Marie. Boy, were they opposites! He couldn't figure out how they could ever work together, but they would. They had to. God had really goofed, putting them together on a team, but David would fix this mistake, too—somehow. Maybe they were already making progress. Maybe not.

"Byte Bitch, huh?" David said as he stood and walked to her side of the table. "I never heard that one. Nice ring, though."

"Right," Marie said—and smiled. Not a forced, tight-lipped smile, but an easy, relaxed one.

Yeah, David thought, *we are making progress.*

6

Bomb with a Capital *B*

DAVID SHOVED all of God's journals to one end of the long table and sat down at the other end. "Okay, what do you need to do first?" he asked Marie.

"You mean *we*, don't you?" Marie corrected.

Oh, she's pushing it, David thought. "Yeah, right. We."

"Well, first we need to establish our arguments— you know—our reasons, or past precedents, for going back. Then we need to research all of the opponent's possible arguments for—"

"Wait a minute," David said. "First things first. Past precedents? How are we going to figure those out?"

"Do you suppose they have a library here?" Marie asked.

"I guess there's one way to find out," David answered. "Let's go down to the coffee bar and ask around." David stood and started walking toward the door.

"David, we don't have time to—"

"Hey! Do I have to do all the work? C'mon—it's research!"

DAVID AND MARIE slid onto tall, tufted vinyl stools at one of the many tall tables that filled the crowded coffee bar overlooking the train station. Within seconds a perky, gum-chewing waitress was at their table.

"What can I getcha?" she asked.

Marie wanted to stick to business. "We're looking for the li—"

"Two iced mocha frappés, please," David said.

"My pleasure!" The waitress smiled and scribbled their order on her pad. "Anything else?"

"No," David said, surveying her starched pink uniform and crisp white apron. He wondered why anyone in heaven would be working instead of hanging out at the beach or going to Magic Mountain. "But can I ask you a personal question?"

"You bet," she said. "Shoot."

"Well, this is heaven and all. Do you have to work here as some sort of punishment or something before you can go and party?"

"Heavens, no!" she laughed. "You see, I died when I was six and I always wanted to be a waitress or ballerina when I grew up. Now I get to do both! When I'm through here I go and perform *Swan Lake* at the theater. Can you beat that?"

"No," David mumbled politely, "I guess not." But his mind reeled. It was all too strange. *This has got to be an episode of* The Twilight Zone *that I missed,* he thought. "Can we get those frappés to go, please?" he asked.

"You bet! They'll be up in a jiff!" the waitress called over her shoulder as she hurried to another table.

"What's the matter, David?" Marie asked. "Don't you want to hang for a while?"

"Let's just ask her where the library is when she comes back, and go. Nardo's bad enough. I don't want this whole place to start growing on me."

David looked down at his watch. The time still showed 1:35 P.M.—the time they had crashed through the guardrail. He tapped the face of the watch a few times with his finger. *We must have been in heaven for hours already,* he thought. *The watch probably broke in the crash.*

"So what do you suppose is happening to our earthly bodies now?" David mused. "Do you think they're slimy yet?"

"Jeez, David! Where do you come up with these things?" Marie asked impatiently.

"Well, you have to admit, it's a little bit of a concern. I mean, if we go back, are we going to show up in first period with worms in our ears and rotting arms and legs falling off in the aisle? I know Mr. Bingsley would give me detention for that."

Marie rolled her eyes. "I don't think it will be a problem, David. I've never heard of that happening before."

"Yeah, well there's always a first time...I *would* like to pop an eye out for Mrs. Graves, though. Bet she couldn't top that."

The waitress returned with their coffees. "You all have a great day, now!"

She is definitely perky, David thought as he reached for his wallet.

"Oh no," the waitress said. "The Boss said this one's on him."

"Thanks," David said. "One more thing—"

"Is there a library around here?" Marie finished.

"Sure thing! It's the first stop that train right over there makes." She pointed to an empty platform. "Next one should be here any minute."

David and Marie grabbed their iced coffees and hurried to the platform to wait. Seconds later a sleek golden train pulled to a whistling stop in front of them. The door slid open, and the first face they saw was Booger's. The others followed excitedly down the steps behind him.

"Yyyow!" Booger wailed his usual tag of approval. "You missed it, buddy!" he said to David. "The waves were"—Booger contorted his face into a look that David recognized as his ecstasy look— "righteous!" Booger finally breathed out.

"I thought you guys were going to the roller coaster," David said.

"Oh, we did. But then we went to the beach. God, he's the bomb," Natalie squealed.

"Who's the bomb?" David asked.

"God!" Natalie repeated.

"Yeah, David," Jason jumped in, "it was so cool. I was out there surfing this perfect wave, and there was God on the same one. He rips, man! Yeah, he's the bomb!"

The bomb? God? David felt his skin prickle and a wild yowl clawed its way up his throat. He pulled his hands down along his face, distorting it. "Excuse me for just one second," he said. He turned and twisted and pulled his shirt up over his face. A loud scream came through the fabric. Slowly David straightened up and lowered his shirt. "Okay," he said without further explanation, "where are you guys off to now?"

"We're going back to the Waiting Room," Mrs. Dunne answered, her hair frizzed out like David had never seen it, "to look through the brochures while we wait for Ernesto."

David hadn't even noticed that Ernesto was missing.

"Where is he?" Marie asked.

"He's at his personal appointment with God. Remember what Leo said? About the personal appointments?" Natalie said excitedly.

David and Marie looked at each other. He knew they were both thinking the same thing. Maybe

Ernesto wouldn't be going back to the Waiting Room. He had done some pretty skanky things.

Natalie continued, bubbling away like a broken sprinkler. "When I have my appointment, I'm gonna ask God if I can join up with the opera company I saw at the Saints Dome!"

"You sing? *Opera?*" David asked, his last word tumbling out of his throat with a squeak.

Natalie blushed and looked down. "Oh yeah... I love *La Bohème.*"

David stared at Natalie. Somehow, with her purple spikes and chains, he had never pictured her singing in an opera with a bunch of angels—and actually liking it! He shook his head. He needed to get out of this place. Fast!

"I hope my appointment's next," Mrs. Dunne said enthusiastically, a big smile spreading across her plump face.

I wouldn't be in such a hurry, David thought. *With all the D's and F's you've given out, your odds might not be any better than Ernesto's.* But because of his last episode with Mrs. Dunne, he carefully kept his thoughts to himself.

The train whistle blew.

"We've gotta go!" Marie said as she pulled David

up the steps of the train. David barely had time to say good-bye before the door slid shut.

They walked down the aisle of the train car and found a seat. Soon they were traveling through the familiar white fog bank.

"Doesn't it kind of tick ya off?" David finally asked.

"More information, David," Marie said impatiently.

"I mean, that God is out whooping it up—surfing and all—while we're busy fighting for our lives."

"Now, that's a statement! Coming from Mr. Responsibility himself. But really, David, don't you suppose God can handle both—surfing and a debate?" Before David could answer, Marie continued, "What I wonder about is, why us? Why is it that only you and I see white fog out the bus and train windows?"

"That's an easy one. You and I aren't ready to go to any of those places that the others see. It's a no-brainer—God made a mistake. We aren't supposed to be here," David answered.

"I don't think so. You heard what Nardo said. God doesn't make mistakes."

"Yeah, right. Then how do you explain ostriches?"

Marie laughed and shook her head. "This is

soooo scary. My life is hanging in the balance, and the guy who is going to argue for me—*my partner*—is completely illogical, undisciplined, and impulsive."

David smiled. "Yeah, don't you love it!"

The train began to slow and a conductor in a tailored blue uniform appeared at the end of the train car. He walked down the aisle, announcing, "Next stop, Last Chance Library!" The conductor stopped next to David's and Marie's seats and pulled a slip of paper from his pocket. "David?" he asked.

"That's right," David answered, still pondering the name of the library.

"Message for you—from God." He handed the folded slip of yellow paper to David and walked away, continuing his singsong announcement as he went down the aisle.

David's heart began thumping as he held the note so he and Marie could read it together.

> *Need any help with the debate?*
> *—God*

David crumpled the note and threw it on the floor. "He's trying to psych us out, ya know. Why would he want to help us?"

"I don't think God has time to play games—"

"Hey, he's eternal. Who has more time than him? I mean, he's probably bored stiff with all these saints hanging around. We're new blood."

Marie looked puzzled, then shook her head. "I have to admit I've never seen anything in the debate guides about opponents helping each other out. Mr. Ferguson never mentioned it. I guess we shouldn't stray from the standard format."

"That's right," David said, pleased that he and Marie were finally agreeing on something.

The train jerked to a halt and they made their way down the aisle to the exit. The same conductor in the blue uniform stood on the platform and offered a hand to Marie as she descended the steps. David eyed him suspiciously.

"What?" he blurted out as he stepped past the conductor. "Did you die when you were six, too?"

7

A Being of the Human Persuasion

AFTER THEIR TELL-ALL session, David thought he knew everything there was to know about Marie. But now as he watched her look of ecstasy—not unlike Booger's—he realized he was just beginning to get to know the girl he had always dismissed with derogatory titles. Miss Frostbite had passion after all.

"C'mon, Marie, don't get too excited. We have work to do," he said, noticing the pink flush moving across her cheeks.

Marie peeled off her navy blue sweater and let it fall carelessly to the floor. "My Lord, David! It's so big!" She breathed heavily.

"Jeez, Marie! It's a library! Libraries are supposed to be big," David said.

"Not like this," Marie answered, mesmerized. She stood in the open foyer, looking up to floor after floor after floor of books. "I've never seen one like *this*. Everything ever written through all of time must be in here. Think of it." She started to walk in a trancelike state toward the first aisle of books.

"Oh no, you don't," David said, grabbing her by the elbow. "The computer catalog is over this way."

Marie lifted her eyebrows in surprise at David's sense of purpose. "If I didn't know better, David, I would say you were almost acting responsibly."

"Me?" David laughed. "Well, if I didn't know better, I'd say you were almost being impulsive—hard to figure, huh?"

The library was crowded. This was another one of those heavenly mysteries David couldn't figure out. He could understand Mrs. Dunne hanging out here, or even other dead teachers, but a lot of the people here looked pretty normal—not teacher types.

There was only one available computer in the long bank of computer catalogs. Marie shook off her wonder of the place and got back to business as she placed her fingers on the keyboard. "Okay," she said, "what do you want me to punch in first?"

"Mistakes, I guess. Yeah, try *God's mistakes,*" he said confidently.

Marie quickly typed in *God's mistakes* and pressed ENTER. The computer hummed and clicked, and the two waited expectantly for a response. The screen politely displayed the message *Still searching* and continued to hum and click. Marie tapped her fingers on the table. David impatiently hit the side of the monitor. Finally another message appeared. *No mistakes found.*

"Jeez!" David said angrily.

"Wait a minute," Marie said. "Let's try this." She typed: *Errors made by God/Yahweh/I Am/Ancient of Days/Alpha and Omega/Prince of Peace.* "That should take care of it," she said.

"We only want God's mistakes," David told her.

"Same difference," Marie said. "All names for the same person. I learned them in Sunday school." She started to press ENTER but David stopped her.

"Wait—type in one more. Sam. *S-A-M.*" Marie wrinkled her face and hesitated. "Just type it," he said again. "It's a hunch."

Marie added *Sam* and pressed ENTER. The computer repeated the process of clicking, humming, and displaying polite messages. David shifted his feet. The wait was not a good sign. Finally the message *Strike two* appeared.

"Damn!" David said as he banged his fists down on the monitor. "I think somebody's jerking our chain!" He pushed Marie aside and began typing.

"What are you doing?" Marie asked.

"I'm typing in *Ostriches*. That should get us somewhere," he said as he pounded the keys.

"David—," Marie started to moan.

"Hey, if this computer won't find us mistakes, we'll find our own." The humming and clicking finally produced some entries. "Here we go! Fourth floor. Six-seventies. Let's go!" David grabbed Marie's hand like she was a two-year-old who might wander off, and he pulled her toward the stairs. When they reached the fourth-floor landing, they were both huffing and puffing.

"Thank goodness ostriches weren't on the zillionth floor," Marie wheezed. "Why are you so certain that ostriches are a mistake?"

"It doesn't take a brain surgeon to figure that one out. They're ugly. They're stupid. And they have wings but they can't fly."

"I think they're kind of cute," Marie said.

"You would. C'mon, this way," David said, still pulling Marie behind him. They found the aisle where the 670s were shelved and began examining the books.

"Here, David. This looks like a good one to start with," Marie said. "It has general facts and history. Let's sit down. I'm still out of breath." They both slid to the floor in the aisle and sat with the book half in David's lap, half in Marie's. Marie, more experienced at research, began expertly skimming the pages for pertinent facts. She mumbled as her fingers moved through the text.

"Wait! Slow down. What are you doing?" David asked, unable to keep up with the swiftly turning pages.

"I'm just looking for some sort of drawback to the bird's physiology."

"It doesn't fly. That's got to be a mistake."

"Afraid not, David," Marie said softly, apparently concerned that losing this point might send David over the edge. "You see, they're native to open, arid country. No trees. They graze on grasses and insects. They have no reason to fly."

"Then what are their damn wings for?"

"They live in really hot country. The mother ostrich uses her wings like an umbrella to give her babies shade. Otherwise they wouldn't survive."

David dropped his head into his hands and stared into his lap as Marie continued to rattle off fact after fact that made the ostrich sound like a better-built machine than a B-52 bomber.

"I suppose I might as well forget about penguins, too," he finally mumbled.

"More information, David."

"Never mind." He sighed.

Marie stared at David, his head lowered in defeat. She closed the ostrich book and nervously tapped its cover. She finally stood up. "There's always the note—the offer of help, I mean. Maybe we should—"

"Focus, Marie! Focus!" David said, using Marie's own motto to emphasize the point. "We've got to stick to our plan. We don't need help from our opponent. Let's just get the books we need for our other arguments and go back to the Waiting Room to work."

Marie smiled. Such as they were—they were still a team.

They scoured various aisles and floors until they

had accumulated an armful of books. David spotted an inconspicuous exit at the end of a long aisle on the sixth floor. "Here, let's go out this way." David opened the door, and he and Marie made their way down the enclosed stairwell. When they reached the bottom, Marie pushed the heavy steel door open and exited first. Before David could follow, he saw Marie's armful of books go flying as she screamed and fell back against the door. David winced as his foot became wedged between the heavy door and the steel frame.

"Open the door, Marie! What's wrong?" David yelled.

"Don't come out, David! Whatever you do, don't come out," Marie screamed, as she shielded her eyes from the terror confronting her. In panic, she pressed all of her weight against the heavy door. David pushed, trying to open it wide enough to yank Marie back in. He expected a giant, blood-sucking tentacle to curl around her legs at any moment and pull her away.

"For God's sake, Marie," he said as he finally rammed the door with his shoulder. Marie's legs gave way and the door flew open. They both went tumbling onto the pavement. David felt his temples throb as the adrenaline pumped through his veins. "Where is it? What?" he said as he quickly turned on his hands and knees in all directions, ready to take on the slimy monster.

He couldn't see anything that was likely to pop their heads off. He crawled over to Marie, who was still shaking. "What is it? What's wrong?" he asked again.

Marie continued to shield her eyes with one hand as she raised a trembling arm and pointed with the other. "Over there!" she shrieked. "Scenery!"

David looked in the direction she was pointing, and could see in the distance a flower-filled meadow dotted with large, lacy oak trees. David rolled onto his back and laughed. "Scenery! Not the dreaded scenery! I thought maybe we had taken one too many flights of stairs down, or maybe the Alien was popping out of someone's chest."

"It's worse, David!" Marie yelled. "Can't you understand that? If we can see scenery like the others do, it means—"

"It doesn't mean anything, Marie," David interrupted, trying to reassure her. "I still haven't changed my mind. I still want to go back. Don't you?"

"Yes, but—"

"No buts. Lighten up. C'mon, I'll show you." He pulled Marie to her feet and started dragging her toward the meadow. "The meadow doesn't mean anything more than the library does, and you didn't freak when you saw *it*."

Marie hesitated, embarrassed that she had made such a scene. "Okay, David, you made your point, but we really don't have time to stroll through a meadow right now. Let's get back to the Waiting Room."

"Hey, we can't research twenty-four seven. If you want to lose the dweeby names, you have to learn to kick back once in a while. Ten minutes won't kill ya."

As David pulled Marie toward the meadow, he wondered himself why he was taking a break when the biggest event of his life—or death—loomed just hours (or was it just minutes?) away. Time seemed to be all out of whack here. Still, taking a break seemed important, even if Marie was a dweeb or a nerd or whatever. He wouldn't have given her a second thought yesterday, but today he wanted to reassure her—to show her how the other half lives.

They walked knee-deep through waving green

grasses until they reached a clearing shaded by a large oak tree. A small stream trickled nearby and wild roses grew along its banks.

"There. See. We're still alive. The scenery didn't kill us." David sat down on the bank of the stream and started to take his tennis shoes off.

"What are you doing now?" Marie asked, concerned that more time would be wasted.

"I want to make sure my little toe is still attached. I think you just about amputated it when you slammed the door." A small dot of blood stained David's white sock.

Marie drew in a deep breath. "I am *so* sorry," she said as she knelt down next to David. "I was just so scared, I wasn't thinking. For a minute there, I just saw everything I ever worked for slipping away. I was afraid I was dead for good, and I would never be able to go back. Are you okay?"

He dipped his foot into the stream. "I'll live. Besides, a bloody toe at least proves I'm not a spook. I don't think angels bleed."

"What makes you so sure you'd be an *angel* if you were dead?" Marie teased.

David looked at Marie and smiled. "Hey, that's

pretty good. One minute of relaxing and you're practically making jokes."

David eyed the profuse yellow and pink blooms that lined the banks. Opportunity was knocking. Even though it was corny and Marie would probably groan, he couldn't pass it by. He reached over and plucked a pink rose. "Your problem, Marie, is that you just don't know how to *stop and smell the roses*. Here," he said as he handed her the rose, "you need the practice. Sniff."

He waited for the groan, but instead her eyes got misty and she turned away. *Oh, God!* He hoped her face wasn't scrunching up like Mrs. Dunne's. What had he said that was so bad?

"Marie, I was just joking. I didn't mean anything by it. Marie?"

"You didn't do anything wrong. It's just that I never..."

David could hear the trembling in her voice and braced himself for the worst. Instead she turned back around, wiping her wet lashes, and smiled.

"Forget it, David. Thanks for the rose." She held it up to her nose and sniffed. "I promise I'll practice—a lot."

8

A Promise
Made...

THOUGH IT wasn't natural for him, David struggled
to be quiet on the train ride back to the Waiting
Room. He still couldn't quite figure out what it was
he had said that had made Marie start leaking back
at the meadow, and he couldn't afford to alienate her
now. He hated needing *anyone,* but he had to admit
it—he needed her help. He was fast on his feet—
good at quick comebacks—sometimes even master-
ful at bull, but he couldn't rely entirely on those
skills for this debate. It was too important. He
needed Marie's research talents and her ability to
stay focused on a goal—no matter what. Definitely
not his specialty.

He ventured an innocent, neutral question. "What time do you have?" he asked.

"I don't know," Marie answered. "My watch must have broken in the crash. It still says one thirty-five. But it's light out—it can't be very late."

David watched as Marie periodically held the pink rose up to her nose and sniffed. *Jeez,* he thought, *she really takes that practice stuff seriously.*

The train squealed to a halt, and they shuffled through the crowds back to the Waiting Room. David reached past Marie and grabbed the door-knob. *"I'll* go in first this time," he said. "You never know what kind of scenery might be lurking behind a door."

"Aaaaaah!" David screamed as he went through the door. Marie thought he was teasing and pushed past him, but then she realized his scream was genuine.

"I think I'm gonna be sick," David whispered to her. They watched as grass skirts swished this way and that. Nardo was leading the group in a conga around the table, with Mrs. Dunne bringing up the rear, her swinging hips posing a danger to all in the room.

"Hey, David! You're back!" Jason called.

David was relieved when the group abandoned the dance and came over to talk to him and Marie. "What are you still doing here?" David asked. "I thought you'd be gone by now, exploring something else."

"Oh, we haven't been here long," Jason said. "We're just waiting for Ernesto."

"Still?" David said. He and Marie exchanged their knowing look again. "Maybe you guys should just go on without him," he suggested. "You don't want to waste all your time around—"

Booger exploded with a laugh. The tropical drink he had been sipping came spraying out his nose. "Who has more time than us, man? We're dead."

"Thanks, Booger," David said as he wiped the spray from his shirt. "What I was trying to say before you gave me a shower was that—" David was interrupted once again when the door behind him opened.

"Ernesto!" Natalie cheered.

David swung around. Ernesto filled the doorway. He practically glowed. He wore a white leather jacket, a white T-shirt, and white jeans. He smiled and held his arms out to his friends. "Check it out, man. Are these threads cool or what?" he said.

Natalie ran and threw an arm around his shoulders and Jason gave him a high five. David stared with his mouth open.

"Did you go shopping, Ernesto?" Marie tried to say casually.

Ernesto laughed. "Heck, no. God gave me these." He straightened the collar of his jacket and strutted into the middle of the room. "Yeah, me and God got to talking, and he thought I'd be pretty good at delivering messages, so I'm going to be hanging out with this dude called Gabriel for a while. He wears white stuff like this, too. Not bad, huh?" Ernesto proudly pulled on the sleeves of his jacket.

"Oh, I almost forgot," he added. "I have my first message to deliver." He slowly pulled a yellow slip of paper from his pocket and held it between his two fingers like it was a cigarette. He raised his dark brown eyes to David's and smiled. "It's for you."

David felt that familiar rubbery feeling in his knees. He hated notes, but he tried to imitate

Ernesto's chilly poise. He coolly lifted the paper from his fingers and read it.

Need any pointers
for the debate?
　　—God

David's calculated calm disappeared, and he crumpled the note and threw it on the table.

"What's the matter, David?" Ernesto asked. "Did Mrs. Graves find you way up here? Is she after you for not making it back to class?"

David didn't answer Ernesto. Instead he turned to the others and said, "Well, everybody's here now. I guess you can all go. Me and Marie have some work to do." It was all the encouragement needed to send everyone noisily shuffling out the door.

As he went past David, Jason pulled his best friend aside so Marie couldn't see, and contorted his face into a grotesque mask. "You're not turning into a geek or something, are you?" he whispered. "You know, all work and no play? Why don't you come with us?"

"Just 'cuz I'm hanging out with Marie doesn't mean I'm a geek, Jason. She isn't either, really. Not like we thought, anyway. Besides, you saw the board. The debate is tomorrow, and I can't weasel out of this one," David whispered.

Jason leaned closer. "I'm not asking you to weasel out of anything. I just want to hang with you for a while. We're buddies, right? C'mon."

David sighed and shook his head. "I can't, bro. Not right now."

"Jason!" Natalie called from the hallway.

"I gotta go. Maybe later?" Jason asked hopefully.

David nodded, but he knew there would be no later. He stared at his best friend walking away. He could see Jason. He could touch Jason. But his friend was as far away from him as east is from west, as dead is from alive, as geeky is from cool. He wanted to bolt from the room, to catch up with Jason, playfully punch him a few times, zoom in on some babes and work their magic. He wanted to flush the debate and have fun with his friends. But the pull to go back was stronger than the urge to party, so he slowly closed the door and turned to face Marie. He waited for her to say something very efficient, very methodical. Something in computerese.

But she just stood there sniffing the pink rose, so he said, "C'mon, we've wasted enough time as it is. Let's get to work."

Marie set the rose aside at one end of the long table and sat down with David at the other end. "Okay. Argument number one," she said. "God made a mistake. We can't use the ostrich for a past precedent, so what's our angle?"

David leaned over the table and rubbed his temples with his fingers. He didn't have an answer. Wasn't that Marie's job? Give him the meat, and he'd add the dressing. He leaned back in his chair and wondered if Jason and the others were on the train yet.

"What about all these journals Nardo brought over?" Marie said. "Should we look through them?"

"You mean the *opponent's* journals?" David grunted. "I don't care what Nardo br—" He paused and his eyes opened wide. "That's it!" David yelled. "Nardo's journal!"

"What are you talking about?" Marie asked.

"Remember on the bus? That dumb little spiral notebook Nardo kept looking at? Those weren't our names in there. Someone else is supposed to be dead right now. We need that journal. That's hard evidence!"

"How are we going to get it? I don't think he's just going to hand it over."

"Why not? This is heaven. Isn't honesty a policy or something like that up here? I'll go find Nardo."

As soon as David stood up to leave, the door opened. Nardo entered, the grass skirt still tied around his waist.

"I have a message for you," he said, and pulled a folded yellow slip of paper from his pocket.

"Let me guess," David said. "From your boss?" David didn't feel rubbery or weak as he snatched the note from Nardo's hand. He only felt irritated as he read the slip of paper.

> *Nah. Won't work.*
> *You might find my*
> *journals helpful, though.*
> *—God*

David slowly ripped the note into tiny pieces and then carefully stuffed them back into Nardo's pocket and patted it. He smiled at Nardo and said calmly, "Your journal. The one you had on the bus. I want it."

Nardo smiled, clasping his hands in front of him, looking slightly embarrassed. "Why, I just don't know what to say! My journal? You want to see *my* journal? It would be an honor! I'll get it right over to you as soon as I'm done copying it." He started to run back out the door, like an excited author who had just been discovered.

"Wait a minute!" David stopped him. "What do you mean 'copying'?"

"Oh, I misplaced my glasses a few days ago, and I'm afraid I made some egregious errors in writing down some of my orders—you know, misspelled names, uneven margins—that sort of thing. Like you, for instance—writing down *Jones* instead of *James*—the way God had it. But I have my glasses back and I'm correcting everything now. I'll have it to you in a jiffy!" He raced excitedly out the door.

Marie closed her eyes and covered her ears, apparently bracing herself for David's reaction. A loud crash echoed through the room . . . and then silence. She opened her eyes to see David calmly returning to his seat across from her. Behind him a folding chair was sprawled across the floor.

"Feel better?" she asked.

"Much," he answered. "In fact, I'm practically delirious. I get to read Nardo's page-turning journal. I can hardly wait."

The two of them sat silently, staring at the collection of materials that littered the table. God's journals. Books from the library. Travel brochures. Half-drunk tropical drinks with colorful paper umbrellas decorating them. Soon Nardo's journal would contribute to the clutter. David didn't know where to start.

"So God doesn't make mistakes," Marie finally blurted out. "That doesn't mean we can't move on to argument number two."

Good, David thought. *Focus.* Yeah, he needed Marie. "So what is argument number two?" he asked.

Marie rolled her eyes. "Past precedents. Remember? God has sent people back before—he can do it again. Here." She pulled a book from the pile they had borrowed from the library and tossed it to David. "You look through that one, and I'll start with these."

David turned the book over in his hands and read the title, *My First Trip to Heaven.* He opened the thin book to the title page. It was by some guy named Lazarus. David began reading. Within a short time he had accomplished the near-impossible. Something he never did at school. He read the whole book in one sitting—no breaks—no Cliffs Notes. Cover to cover. He slammed the book down on the table, making Marie jump.

"This is it!" he said. "This has got to be it!"

"More information, David," Marie said as she caught her breath.

"This dude was even deader than us! Four days! They had already sealed him up in this cave—funeral and everything. I mean, this guy was *stinking,* and God sent him back." David stood up and euphorically paced about the room. "We haven't even been up here for one whole day yet—that should give us some leverage."

"That's good, David," Marie said excitedly. "I found something, too, about this guy from a city called Nain. He wasn't dead for four days, but they were already marching him around in his coffin when God brought him back. Can you imagine the look on everyone's faces when he popped up? And then there was this twelve-year-old girl, daughter of this guy named Jairus—I don't know how long she had been dead, but everyone was sitting around her crying, and God grabbed her hand and she got up and ate lunch!"

"Dead one minute, eating a Big Mac the next. Awesome!" David said. "It sounds like the Big Kahuna does this sort of thing all the time. So we should have no problem—no problem at all! Right?"

"Maybe. Except that—"

"What do you mean *maybe*? This is going to be a slam dunk."

"But, David—"

"Forget the *maybe*s and the *but*s, would you?" David sat back down and leaned toward Marie. "So what do I do? Just get up during the debate and read off a list of the names of who he's sent back before?"

The color drained from Marie's face. "David, I know you never showed up at any of the debate competitions, but didn't you at least listen at the meetings?"

David frowned and leaned back. *Why does she have to get so technical?* "No, I didn't listen much. I was just putting my time in."

Marie slammed her fists down on the table. "Well, it was a big waste of time! Jeez-Louise, David!"

David could only guess that a ticking time bomb had finally exploded. Marie stood up, her chair tumbling over behind her. She threw her hands into the air and started yelling to the ceiling, to the walls, to everything but David, as she paced about the room. "I can't believe it! My whole life is in the hands of PeeWee Herman! I'm losing everything! Everything! All my hard work was for nothing!" The tears started to flow, but she continued to rave. " 'Do you play football?' Noooo. 'Do you wrestle?' Noooo. 'I debate.' I *debate*! How *could* you, David! You might as well have said you were an astronaut! God help me!" She fell back against the wall, sobbing.

David wasn't sure what train had just passed through, but he sure hadn't seen it coming. He was at a loss. A complete loss. For once he had nothing to say. There *was* nothing to say. Marie was right about everything. He had blown it. Not only was he screwing up his future, but he was pulling Marie down with him. His bull had landed them both in a big pile of...

"Marie," he started to stay, but then he set his words aside and acted on his instincts instead. He walked over and put his arms around her and held her as she cried. All the saved-up tears a computer could ever hold came pouring out.

"It's going to be okay. I promise," he whispered.

David closed his eyes and stroked Marie's hair. There was no question now that the microchip had feelings, but the goof-off—did *he* have what it would take to see this thing through? He didn't know. He just didn't know.

9
A Trick?

MARIE WIPED her cheeks with her hands and began straightening the piles of clutter on the table once again. "David, I'm really sorry. I don't know what came over me. I said a lot of things that I didn't really mean. It was just a lot of emotion. All those words just sort of jumped out before I could think them through. It's not like me to—"

"Stop apologizing," David interrupted, trying to minimize the whole encounter. "You were human. Normal." Marie smiled softly, repeating the words *human* and *normal*. David continued. "You were right, too. I did screw up. But I'm going to make it right—somehow. Now let's get back to work."

It's going to be okay. I promise. David's words haunted him unlike any others he had ever said. When he had whispered them into Marie's ear, he had meant them, but he didn't know how he would ever make them true.

They sat down and looked at their meager notes. *Argument number one* had been crossed off. *Argument number two—past precedents—* had a few names jotted down next to it, and *Argument number three* was blank.

David stared absently across the room and mumbled, "Number three. I just want to...I just want to go back."

"Should I write that down?" Marie asked.

"No," David said. "It may be true, but it's not very impressive. We've got to think big. Just leave it blank for now. Maybe we can come up with some more people for number two. That seems to be our best bet right now."

Marie was starting to reach for another library book when the door opened. It was Nardo, returning with his prized journal.

"See. I told you I wouldn't be long. Here it is," he said happily, "all corrected, of course. I hope you enjoy it!" Nardo proudly handed the notebook to David.

"Thanks," David said as he reached for it, but then he spotted a wedge of yellow paper peeking from Nardo's pocket. *Jeez! Another note.* David thought fast.

"Hey, Nardo, would you mind showing Marie where the Coke machine is while I look through your journal? I'm really thirsty."

"My pleasure!" Nardo said.

"But, David—," Marie started to say, a puzzled look on her face.

"Please, Marie," David insisted.

Marie gave in with a shrug.

David turned back to Nardo. "Thanks, bro," he said, giving Nardo a pat on the back and a few playful punches, like he did with Jason. In the midst of the interplay, he deftly slipped the paper from Nardo's pocket and into his own. He couldn't explain it, but he just didn't want to read it with Marie in the room.

Nardo escorted Marie out, and when the door was firmly shut behind them, David pulled the slip of paper from his pocket. He sat down to read it.

A little tidbit to help you out. Lazarus will tell you he didn't even want to go back. In fact, he had already started a bagel shop up here but went back as favor to me. You see, I was starting this new campaign at the time, and I was making a point. He was helping me out. Same with the others.

You might want to move on to your next argument.

Just want to help.

—God

David stared at the wall. *Damn!* But he wasn't cursing God—he was cursing himself. Marie had tried to tell him. She knew there was a flaw in their argument, but he wouldn't listen.

Maybe... but... and then he had cut her off. He hadn't *listened*. He never did. That was his problem: He only exercised his mouth. His ears were practically disabled. Now he was going to have to tell Marie that their second argument wasn't going to fly, either. Just like she had tried to warn him. *It's going to be okay. I promise.* That stupid promise!

David wished that the Coke machine was on the other side of heaven so it would take them a couple of millennia to return. He leaned back in his chair and ran his fingers through his hair. He closed his eyes. *It's going to be okay. I promise.* Who was he to promise anything? And what was so bad about being in heaven, anyway? After all, they could have ended up in that *other* place. Maybe he should just give up. Wave the white flag.

He heard a loud bang and opened his eyes, but it was only one of the journals. He must have bumped the table and knocked it to the floor. He leaned over to pick it up. Genesis. He wondered if this was some kind of manual for Sega Genesis. Was God into video games, too?

He stared at the plain black book for a long time. The opponent's journal. Wasn't this the one Nardo had said to read first? It was probably a trick. He tossed the book back onto the table and dropped his head into his hands. He had to think. He had to come up with something quick—before Marie came back. Leaning over, he felt as puky as if he were leaning over a toilet. Not the barf kind of puky, but the empty kind when all the barf is out. He was empty—not a thought in his head.

"David?"

He jerked his head up. He hadn't heard Marie

come in. She held two cans of Coke in her hands. "What are you doing?" she asked.

"Nothing. I mean, thinking. You know, just thinking," David said, caught off-guard and stumbling for words. He didn't like Marie seeing him in this weakened state. Last time he had let down his guard, she had stabbed him royally.

"Well, you don't look good at all." She set the Cokes down and grabbed his hand. "C'mon," she said. "What you need is a break—a change of scenery."

David wouldn't budge from his chair. "There isn't time, Marie. I have too much work that I—"

"What? Is ten minutes going to kill ya?" She smiled and reached for the rose on the table with her free hand. "Your problem, David, is you just don't know how to *stop and smell the roses.* Let's go!" She yanked on his hand and pulled him to the door.

10

Just Naked People and Big Boats

EVEN THOUGH he knew his watch was broken, David couldn't help but nervously glance at it every few minutes. He couldn't believe it was still light out—it seemed like they had been in heaven for days.

"Would you relax!" Marie scolded as they strolled through the busy train station.

"That's easy for you to say. If I end up blowing this debate, I'm the one who has to live for the rest of eternity knowing I royally screwed up someone else's life. I'll be known as the Eternal Flake."

Marie smiled, and brushed the rose that she still carried along her cheek. "Better that than the Eternal Dweeb."

She stopped and faced him. "David, you may as

well know, my life was screwed up long before I got here. I may have had a 4.7 grade-point average, but about the only things I could relate to were books and time schedules. I wasn't just *given* all of those names—I earned them. I was Miss Frostbite because I wanted to be. I didn't want to need anyone. Even if we never go back, I—"

David didn't like the way the conversation was turning. "Marie, I made you a promise and I—"

"David! You're not getting the message! We *all* need help now and then. I needed help. Your help. I'm only just beginning to see how much I was missing—and I still have a long way to go. A leopard doesn't change its spots overnight. But win or lose, I'm *glad* I was your partner. I think if I were to go back I'd be a better person—because of you."

"Oh yeah, sure. Everybody's better for knowing me," David teased.

Marie playfully hit David in the stomach with her hand that held the rose. Pink petals went scattering to the floor. David saw the dismayed look on Marie's face.

"Hey, don't worry about it. No problem. I'm sure there is some dead six-year-old around here who always wanted to carry a broom and dustpan. They'll be along to clean it up."

"It's not that," Marie said. She stooped and began placing the loose petals in her cupped hand.

"Marie," David said impatiently, "it's just a rose. Leave it."

"It's not just a rose to me, David." She continued to place the petals methodically in her palm.

Seeing she could not be swayed, David stooped to help her. "I don't know what the big deal is," he said. "There will be other roses."

Marie smiled and shook her head. "Not for me, David. Not for Her Royal Dweebness. Nerds aren't generally the target of rose deliveries. This is the first and probably last rose anyone will ever give to me."

What a butthead he was. No wonder she got all misty when he first gave it to her. He should have known she wasn't sniffing it all the time just because it smelled good. He wished he could promise her there would be other roses, but he didn't want to make any more promises he couldn't keep. Instead he changed the subject as he dropped the petals he had gathered into her hands.

"Look over there," he said, pointing to where a crowd had gathered around some street entertainers, or in this case, train-station entertainers. "Let's go see what's up. Maybe someone's juggling halos."

They pushed through the crowd until they could see what the excitement was all about. There were indeed some jugglers—three of them—and one of them was Booger! They were all juggling and balancing a variety of things—large colorful balls, hats, bricks, and oranges. But no halos. Booger balanced a large plastic pitcher of water on his head as he alternately juggled the items with other members of the team. For the second time in one day, David was at a loss for words. Like Honors Bio, this was the last place he expected to see Booger.

He and Marie watched as the juggling team worked with split-second precision, tossing fruit among themselves as each one juggled items of his own, trusting and depending on each member to deliver the goods. For the first time, David wondered what else he didn't know about Booger.

David called out to him. "Hey, Booger! Awesome!" They were only three words, but David immediately knew they were three words too many, as Booger turned his head to David's familiar voice.

The rest was a slow-motion nightmare. The finely tuned machine was now a ballerina wearing army boots; David had thrown a wrench into the interlocking cogs. Fruit smashed to the floor, bricks careened into the crowd, and the pitcher full of water flew from Booger's head like a gooney bird from a runway. David thought he could dodge it, but it seemed to have the same homing capabilities as a pigeon and landed squarely on his chest, water drenching his shirt and pants and running down into his shoes.

David stood with his arms outstretched, looking at the dripping mess.

"Yyyow!" Booger laughed. "Look at you!"

"This is the second time today that you've given me a shower, Booger!" David scowled.

"Well, take a hint, bro." Booger laughed again, and then went about picking up wayward fruit and pitchers before rejoining his team.

"Well, do you at least feel refreshed now?" Marie teased.

David's silent look of contempt answered Marie's question. "Let's go," he said, trying to gather together what little pride and dignity he still had left, but as he walked away, the squishy-squashy sound of his own soggy shoes penetrated the scowl, and they both erupted into laughter.

"Well, it's been a real *thrill* and all," David said, "but I think we should go back to the Waiting Room now—remember? The debate?"

Marie agreed, and they walked back silently to the Waiting Room. David breathed deeply. He wanted to tell Marie about the last note—that their argument for past precedents wasn't looking good, either—but it was easier just to remain silent. He couldn't have cared less about Marie's feelings yesterday, but today...he didn't want to let her down. She wasn't Her Royal Dweebness anymore.

He'd think of something.

Somehow.

They stopped at the coffee bar on the way back and got two frappés to go, and except for the sucking sound of David's soggy shoes, they continued to walk silently. The Waiting Room was empty when they returned, and David wondered if the room had been set aside just for them. Surely throughout all the earth someone else had died in these past hours, and yet no one else was passing through. As Marie began sifting through their collection of materials, he wondered about other things, too. What were his parents doing right now? Did they know? Was he stinking like Lazarus yet? If he were to go back, how would they stuff all his intestines back into him? Would he be able to raise his D in English Lit to a C? And for the first time, he wondered if there were still any openings on the West City League baseball team.

A loud bang ripped him from his thoughts. It was that dumb journal again. Genesis.

"Sorry," Marie said. "I guess I must have knocked it off the table."

David leaned over to pick it up and saw the edge of a yellow note peeking from the pages. He pulled it out and read it.

> *It's really not*
> *a bad read.*
> *—God*

David balked and shook his head. "With all the notes this guy likes to write, he never would have made it in school—or he would have spent a lot of time in detention."

Marie looked up from her book. "What?" she asked.

"Nothing," David answered. He leaned forward

to throw the book back onto the table, but then he stopped and leaned back instead, the journal firmly in his grasp. What did he have to lose? He opened it to the first page.

It was pretty hairy stuff. No amoebas in here. Mrs. Dunne would have shuddered. There were naked people running around in a garden, and angels with flaming swords. It didn't sound much like Nardo. And there was some guy who built boats the way God built centipedes—he didn't know when to stop. Yeah, he'd give God this much—it wasn't a bad read.

"What are you reading?" Marie asked, in between her research books.

"Just this journal." David held it up so she could read the spine.

Marie raised her eyebrows. "The *opponent's* journal?"

"That's right," David said. "I figure I have nothing to lose."

"Find anything?"

"Nah. Not yet. Just some naked people and big boats."

Marie sighed. "Well, don't give up. I'm afraid I'm not getting anywhere." Marie hesitated for a moment. "I might as well tell you now, David, that I don't think we're going to get too far with that past-precedents argument. You see—"

"Yeah, I know. None of them really wanted to go back—it was just a favor they did. Some new campaign or something." David leaned back in his chair and let out a long groan.

It will be okay. I promise. He hated nags, especially when he was the one doing the nagging. He sat back up in his chair and looked into Marie's warm brown eyes. "I'm sorry, Marie, for getting you into this. I should have said 'detention.' "

Marie laughed, then offered her customary response to David's incomplete thoughts. "More information, David."

"When Nardo asked me what I did," he explained, "I should have said 'detention.' I have lots of experience at that. I'm sure I could have beaten God at sitting it out. I even know how to make it entertaining. Dead-on spitwads. Pencil arrows in the ceiling. Loud obnoxious noises. Sometimes even ones that smell so the teacher will dismiss you early."

Marie grinned and said softly, "But we can't look back, David, can we? You didn't say 'detention.' You said 'debate.' Besides, 'sitting it out' isn't really much fun. Wouldn't you rather take your chances debating? I would."

"Thanks, Marie," he said.

Somehow. Some way. He wouldn't give up. Not this time.

He opened the journal where he had left off, and continued to read.

From big boats it moved on to more wild stuff. A skyscraper named Babel that was so high, just looking at it would give you a nosebleed. Then there was some lady who just couldn't let go of the past and, looking back, she turned into a block of Morton salt. Pretty creative. And now he was reading about some jerk named Jacob who was scheming to steal his brother's inheritance.

Okay. So it wasn't a bad read. God was right up there with Stephen King and Tom Clancy, but how was any of this going to help him? David threw the journal onto the table.

"Giving up?" Marie asked.

David thought about her question. Was he giving up? It would be so much easier. Jason had probably scoped out all of the best places by now. All he had to do was walk out that door and let the good times roll. No homework. No detention. No Mrs. Graves.

It's going to be okay. I promise. There was that stupid promise! He had promised things a hundred times before. *Yeah, I'll clean my room. Yeah, I'll study for the test. Yeah, their parents will be home. Yeah, I'll keep my mitts off the microphone. Yeah, yeah, yeah.* Why was this promise rattling around in his head, when the others had been a puff of air breezing through? Why did it feel like his last chance at everything?

No. He wasn't giving up—for now.

"Just stretching," he said, and he picked the journal back up.

He read more about Jacob's travails. Cheating his brother. Running off to hide. And then David came to a part that made him sit up straight in his chair. He shook his head. It was unbelievable! After everything this guy had done, he had the nerve to *wrestle God*! Really wrestle him. Down and dirty wrestling. All night long and into the next morning. This jerk just wouldn't give up! Even when God knocked his hip out of joint, he wouldn't stop until God gave him what he wanted. Talk about balls!

David jumped up and snapped the journal shut, startling Marie again.

"Honestly, David! Can't you—"

David grabbed both of her arms. "Marie! Do you have a date for the prom?" he asked excitedly.

Marie could hardly answer, her confusion stumbling her words. "No—but—what on earth are you—"

David cut her off again. "Then you're going with me!" He let go of her arms and ran out the door, but then poked his head back in. "And make sure your dress isn't strapless! I'm going to buy you the biggest rose corsage you ever saw!"

11

Junkyard Dog

"NARDO!" David yelled as he walked down the hallway. "Nardo! Where are you?" He reached the end of the hallway and entered the cavern of the train station, still gripping God's journal in his hand. He was oblivious to the stares he drew as he continued to call out Nardo's name. He was focused. Nothing could deter him from his goal.

"Nardo! I need to talk to you! Nardo!"

He searched the chattering faces of the coffee bar for Nardo's peculiar grin, but all the smiles were unfamiliar. He knew he should have insisted on a bleepin' beeper number! He walked back in the other direction and felt a tap on his shoulder. He turned around and saw the grin he had been looking for.

"Nardo! I've been looking all over for you! I need to talk to God!"

Nardo's grin widened to a smile, "Mr. James, I think I already covered this with—"

"Listen, Nardo," David said, as he poked Nardo's chest with his pointed finger. "I remember what you said, but I'm not going to roll over and die for you like I did on the bus. I don't care what you have to do—chalk it up to my 'personal appointment' if you want, but I—"

"You just don't understand how—"

"No! You're the one who doesn't get it. Read my lips, Leee-ohh. I'll say it for you real slowww. *I want to talk to God now!*"

Nardo straightened his back, his nose slightly tilted up. "Well!" He harrumphed. "I guess you'd better come with me, then." He spun on his heel and started walking away. David followed closely behind.

When Nardo reached the hallway that jutted off of the train station—the hallway that led to the Waiting Room—he turned.

"Wait a minute!" David yelled as he continued

to trail behind Nardo. "I'm not going back to the freakin' Waiting Room! I don't—"

Nardo stopped and wriggled all over. "Mr. James," he said, "there are *other* rooms down this hallway. Would you *please* just follow me."

Nardo walked past the Waiting Room and stopped at the door just beyond it. "Wait here," he said as he wrapped his hand around the doorknob.

"Here?" David said in disbelief. "You mean all this time God was just in the next room? Right next to me?"

"That's right. He was always that close, David." Nardo gently tapped on the door a few times. "Hey, Sam, this James kid is all hot and bothered," he called through the door. "Can you see him?"

Sam? Sam! "Yes!" David whispered as he jerked his hand into a triumphant fist. The affirmation of his hunch gave David a quick boost of confidence.

There was no answer from within, and Nardo cracked the door slightly and poked his head inside. David noticed a gentle breeze slipping through the crack, ruffling Nardo's thin wisps of hair. When Nardo withdrew his head from the door, he held a small yellow slip of paper in his hand.

"I think this is for you," Nardo said. David

snatched the note from Nardo's fingers and read it aloud.

> *It's time for the debate.*
> *Meet you at the arena*
> *by the marquee.*
> *Now.*
>
> *Good luck,*
> *—God*

"Now?" David turned frantically to Nardo. "No! You don't understand! *He* doesn't understand. I don't want to debate him anymore! I just need to talk to him!"

"Talk, talk, talk," Nardo muttered. "You just seem to be stuck on that, don't you? But the debate *is* on, and God *is* waiting. Shall we go, Mr. James?"

"But Marie!" David protested. "I need Marie!"

"No," Nardo reminded him. "The debate is just between you and God. Marie has finished her part. Come along."

David's confidence fell with a thud, and he felt his knees turn to rubber, the rubber to mush. *Give up! Give up! This game's too big for you!* But David pushed the mush forward with whatever strength was still lingering in his legs. *I can't give up!* He wobbled down the hallway behind Nardo, feeling the mush turn back to rubber, and amazingly, the rubber back to bone.

David followed Nardo until they reached the edge of a large arena, semicircular in shape, with a round stage as its focal point. The small stage looked up to the thousands of seats on one side, and out onto the train station on the other side. Why hadn't he seen this arena before? He looked at the seats filled with hippies, waitresses, mimes, jugglers, and, of course, angels. Hundreds of angels. Maybe thousands. Thousands of freakin' angels with fluttering wings.

He was going to throw up. He was certain of it. Now he would not only be the Eternal Flake, he would be the Barfing Eternal Flake. Nardo guided him down the hundreds of steps that led to the small stage at the bottom. The debating stage. David looked down at his dirty tennis shoes, concentrating on navigating each step, concentrating on his stomach, concentrating on his new name. Barfing Eternal Flake.

It was the walk of a lifetime. David couldn't bring himself to look to his destination. He could only look at one agonizing step at a time. Was there some six-year-old in heaven who always wanted to clean up barf?

He took the final step down onto the stage, afraid to lift his eyes from his ragged shoes. But then he remembered Marie and his resolve, and he forced his gaze upward. Where *was* his opponent? At first he saw only two empty white chairs gracing the center of the stage, but as his gaze continued to rise—he saw. He stared at the back of a large figure standing on the edge of the open precipice that faced out on the train station.

David could see all that the figure saw—the comings and goings of trains, new arrivals in other waiting rooms—but even more than that. He could see beyond the train station. He saw a crowded city, an empty plain, a nest of robins. He saw pyramids that shone in the sun, not yet decayed by centuries of blowing sand. He saw water covering a very small planet and a rainbow shining above it all. He saw dust being breathed into life, tenderly shaped by a craftsman, lovingly allowed to take its own form. Laws of time and space seemed to yield to another law. Perspective flowed back, forth, and around, like the incoming tide on a shore. David no longer noticed the thousands of spectators poised in their seats, their wings beating in anticipation. Instead he noticed the breeze that had ruffled Nardo's hair now ruffled his own, but more than just his hair—it seemed to penetrate his skin; it was a warm fluid breeze that sought to envelop his very bones.

He could only see the back of the figure, but David's eyes fixated on the presence.

Then he remembered—there was something he wanted to say. He felt like his tongue had swollen to the size of a giant zucchini and was certain his words would gurgle out with the finesse of a clogged drain being plunged, but somehow...his focus remained. He cleared his throat to speak, and the figure turned around, the two-second revolution becoming an eternity in itself.

For the briefest moment David expected to be vaporized and become so much dust sprinkling to the floor, and then he thought perhaps his knees would give way after all. And finally he just waited to see if God with a capital G looked like the sound of thunder, like the chiseled granite of David's small imagination.

David looked into God's eyes, and he felt as though he were tumbling into a warm pool of water. He was immersed, blanketed. He forgot about the debate, the spectators, his death, his friends, even his nemesis, Mrs. Graves. He didn't see cold unfamiliar eyes but Jason's eyes, his best friend's eyes, warm, inviting. He saw Mrs. Dunne's dimpled cheeks, and Marie's intense gaze. He saw Ernesto's unflustered nod, and Natalie's grin with her tongue in her cheek. He even saw Booger. He saw every face he had ever known—and every face he hadn't.

He searched God's face. God was an old friend, someone David had always known, but he was also a stranger. One David had passed on the street, averting his eyes, not wanting to become engaged. The misfit he had dismissed with a casual remark.

And then the sound of thunder became a gentle voice. "Welcome, David," God said as he held his hand out. "Shall we begin?"

It was too weird. Here he was face-to-face with God, shaking his hand. David dropped his hand to his side. He remembered why he was here. Marie. The debate. His life.

"How much time do I have?" David asked.

"What?" Nardo intervened.

David shifted his feet, trying to imitate Ernesto's cool stance, trying to appear in control though every hair on his body prickled like a cornered cat's fur.

"How much time do I have to present my arguments?" he asked again.

"You can take as long as you like," God answered.

Yes! David thought as he closed his eyes and swallowed hard. It was the answer he had hoped for. As much time as he needed.

Nardo dived into his role as moderator and motioned to the chairs. "Please take your seats and we'll begin."

David took the few short steps and stumbled into his chair.

Nardo turned to the crowd and announced, "Welcome to our debate! Today David James will debate God."

A hush ran through the crowd, and in turn made a flutter run through David's stomach. Barfing Eternal Flake. Who else in the entire universe would challenge *God* to a debate? "Even the angels can't believe it!" David muttered as he ran one hand across his wet forehead. He looked down and saw a dark, damp blotch forming on his T-shirt. *Jeez!* Maybe if he was lucky he would just melt into a small sweaty pool, and they would suck him up with a mop-vac.

Nardo continued with the introduction. "The

topic will be 'Should David be allowed to return to his mortal life?' David will present his arguments first, and after each presentation, God will have the opportunity for rebuttal. We ask that you refrain from applause until the end of our program. Thank you." Nardo walked with all the dignity of a moderator to an empty seat in the first row. He sat down and, with an odd expression that hovered somewhere between horror and hysterical laughter, he nodded to David. "You may begin, Mr. James."

David sat there silently, unable to speak, his tongue firmly pasted to the roof of his mouth. Every eye in heaven bore into him, each gaze wildly scattering his thoughts. Trickles of sweat ran down his temples. He fought to organize his scattered thoughts. *A promise. Jason. No, Jacob. Don't give up. Marie. Wrestling. My promise. My promise.*

"I have to go home and feed my dog!" he suddenly blurted out.

Hushed giggles rippled through the arena. Nardo frowned and cleared his throat to restore order. "And?" Nardo prompted David, waiting for the meat of the argument.

"And he's going to be really hungry if I don't feed

him," David answered, unaffected by Nardo's annoyance.

Nardo sighed and turned to David's opponent. "God, do you care to respond?"

God smiled and winked at David. "I left a note for your brother. He'll take care of Duke for you."

Another note. I should have known, David thought.

"Next argument!" Nardo bellowed as he flipped a card on a score chart. David stared at the score: DAVID–0, GOD–1.

David swallowed and offered his next argument. "I forgot my last two hair appointments, and they said if I forget another one they're going to charge me anyway, and my mom will be really ticked off if that happens."

Nardo bristled in his chair. "Now really, Mr. James!" he said as he wriggled all over, but God interrupted the coming tirade.

"It's okay, Leo." He turned to David. "Your appointment is Wednesday, right?"

"Yeah."

"Leo, call and cancel, will you? We don't want Mrs. James to be charged for nothing."

Leo looked straight into David's eyes. "Good as

canceled, Sam!" he said as he flipped another card over. DAVID–0, GOD–2. "Next argument, Mr. James?"

David continued to blurt out any and every argument for his return—because he had *all the time he needed.* He would never give up. By the time he got to his twentieth argument he noticed the trickles of sweat that had accompanied his first arguments had shrunk to mere beads. The flutter in his stomach that had threatened him with eternal embarrassment had quieted. He was ready for more, though the scorecard read DAVID–0, GOD–20.

By the time they reached argument forty-three, David noticed that all signs of annoyance had fled Nardo. The discouraged moderator stared, in a trance, at the two opponents, flipping the scorecard by rote. Angels and hippies had begun to nod off on each other's shoulders, and the only sound that could be heard from the crowd was an occasional snore or a muffled yawn. Only God—*and* David— seemed prepared to go on.

Opportunity knocked and David was on a roll. He jumped up to belt out argument forty-four. The sweat and flutter were distant memories. His knees weren't even made out of bone anymore—they were pure steel—even kryptonite couldn't stop him now.

"Okay," he said as he paced about the stage, "the Forever-Shine wax on my car has a double-your-money-back guarantee if the shine fades within six months. I still have another month to go on that guarantee, and I noticed around the fender that—"

"Mr. James!" Nardo shouted as he jumped up, reclaiming his authority as moderator. "I think you have had all the time you need! As moderator of this debate I must—"

"Wait a minute!" David interrupted, just as ready as Nardo to defend his position. "Before this debate started I asked how much time I had, and God said I had as much time as I wanted! Well, I want more!"

David turned from Nardo to God and the words poured out like water from a drain that had been unclogged. "We can continue with this debate thing if you want, but I'll tell you right now that I'm going to win. I want to go back—no—I *am* going back." David took a deep breath as he stared straight into God's eyes. "You see, I figured out that I'm as good a debater as Jacob was a wrestler, and I'll never give up. Never! Just like him. I don't care if you knock my hip out of joint—or in my case, if my tongue shrivels up and falls out of my mouth! I'll present arguments in sign language if I have to." David looked up to the crowd that had been jerked back awake, sitting silently on the edges of their seats—in awe or terror, David didn't know—but he turned back to God and continued. "I'll be like a junkyard dog with locked jaws. I won't let go. I'll come up with as many arguments as there are days in eternity—and then some! They might be stupid, miserable, and boring, but you and all your heavenly hosts will have to listen to every one—because I have all the time I need and *I'll never give up!*"

David's eyes didn't stray from God's, but he could hear the gasps from angels and the "Oh, man!" from hippies, fearful that the match might continue into the next millennium.

Silent seconds passed but David's eyes didn't waver—and neither did God's. Finally God spoke. "Ya know, David, I think we already heard all your stupid arguments, but you say you have miserable and boring ones, too?"

"That's right," David answered.

God paused again. "You'd be a general pain, huh?"

"Oh no," David said, "a very *specific* pain!"

God turned around and gazed out to the train station, to the ages past, present, and those to come. "You'd *never* give up?" he asked.

"Never," David said confidently.

God turned back around. "Why, David? Only because you think you can wrestle as well as Jacob? Or because your fender is getting dull? Are those the only reasons you won't give up?"

God stared into David's eyes; their gazes locked. David felt the blood that had been surging through his veins draining into his feet. This "revealing stuff" was so hard. Harder than wrestling...but he wasn't going to give up now.

"No," David whispered. This time David turned, looking out to the train station, to the ages past and present. "Not just because of my dull fender, or because I like to wrestle..."

David smoothed back his hair with his hand and turned to face God. He didn't feel puky or rubbery—just naked. "Because I've found that there are lots of things in life that we can give up on besides a fender or a wrestling match or a debate. We can give up on other things—like people. Ones with purple hair. Ones with goofy laughs and dreadlocks...ones who hide behind navy blue cardigans and tight-lipped smiles because they've given up, too. We give up on them by giving them some funny names and then never looking past those. We shut them out of our lives. And sometimes when we give up on others it makes it a whole lot easier to give up on ourselves...and maybe...I guess...I'm just not ready to do that."

Yup. He was naked, all right.

God stared at him, waiting.

David stared back. His voice wobbled. "And if we give up on people—if we give up on ourselves and our dreams—we're as good as dead, even if we've never stepped one lousy foot into heaven."

Argument forty-five seemed to suck all of the air right out of the arena. No one moved. Nardo waited. The angels waited. The hippies waited.

David waited.

He felt himself melting into God's gaze. He no longer felt naked.

God nodded. He turned back around to Nardo. "Flip the cards, Leo."

David watched as Nardo flipped the scorecards on David's side until a W appeared.

"You win, David," God said.

A tremendous cheer rang from the crowd as it rose to its feet to celebrate the victory.

David was caught off-guard. He was still ready to wrestle. "That's it? It's that easy?"

"Easy?" God laughed. "Has it really been *easy*, David?"

David looked into the familiar eyes, his question answered, his awareness reaching in wider circles. David stepped closer to God and whispered, "You never really were my opponent, were you?"

"You're a smart kid, David. You always were. I used to laugh when you were still in your mother's womb and you would hiccup to get her to roll over."

David remembered! A memory that had vanished became clear. A pinched elbow and a hiccupping plea for more room.

"Yes," God went on, "you're a smart kid, David... use it." He nodded his head again in Ernesto's too-cool way. "You can go on back to the Waiting Room now. We'll send you on your way before you know it."

"One more question," David said. "Me and Marie. Putting us on the same team was no mistake, was it?"

"Like I said, David: You're a smart kid. But for

the record—no." God smiled Mrs. Dunne's dimpled smile and added, "It was no more of a mistake than a three-hundred-pound bird that can't fly."

David smiled. "Well, I guess I'll see you around, then," he said, moving toward the steps.

"Sooner than you think, David," God answered as he winked. "Oh, David, one more thing. Check in with me now and then. Just to talk. Like you used to when you were little. Not this wrong-number stuff I've been getting from you. You know, 'God this!' 'Jesus that!' And then when I pick up the line's dead. If you call my name—mean it. We'll talk, okay?"

David nodded his head. "We'll talk."

Nardo resumed his role as moderator. Standing before the crowd, he announced with a theatrical flounce, "Debate goes to ... David!"

The crowd went wild with cheers again; but ironically, leaving the stage now created the same rubber in David's legs that arriving had done just hours earlier. God gave him a final nod, and David found the courage to proceed up the steps of the aisle. The mimes, the waitresses, every assortment of travelers shook his hand as he progressed up the stairs. Angels gave him low and high fives, and hippies gave him hugs. The celebration was deafening, and David wondered if their merriment came just from sheer relief that the debate was over.

He shook the last hand and stepped from the arena.

David walked with quickening steps toward the Waiting Room. The din of the celebration, the victory, still rang in his ears. He suspected that it always would.

Yeah, Natalie and Jason were right. God was the bomb. It had just taken David awhile to know what that meant. He finally made it to the Waiting Room and reached for the doorknob. This was it. He was finally going back. He started to turn the knob, but something caught his eye at the end of the hallway. It was the group. The goof-offs, plus one—Mrs. Dunne. He hadn't seen them at the debate, and now it looked like they were on their way to some other destination. David ran to catch up with them—just to say good-bye.

"Jason! Nat! Wait up! Did you see the debate?" he asked.

"Ah, sorry, bro. We missed it," Jason said as he gave David a low five. "But you're just in time! We're on our way to see the Three Jays."

"The Three Jays?" David asked, the name unfamiliar to him.

"Yeah," Natalie said, "Jimi, Janis, and John. They're in concert."

"They were big in the sixties," Mrs. Dunne added, "and now they've formed a new group up here, and they're even bigger."

"Yeah, I heard they really rip. Let's go. We want to get a good seat," Ernesto said.

Booger laughed. "Hey, *all* the seats at the Saints Dome are good!"

Jason swung his arm around David and started to pull him along with the group toward the train platform.

"Wait a minute, you guys," David said as he planted his feet. "The concert sounds great, but I'm going to have to catch the Three Jays later. A lot later. I won the debate. I'm going back."

The chatter and laughter of the group stopped.

"Really?" Jason finally asked.

"Yeah. Really. In just a few minutes, in fact, so I'm just here to say good-bye."

Mrs. Dunne stepped closer. "David, as long as you're going that direction, would you tell the rest of the class that their homework won't be due until

Tuesday? I figure an extra day is the least I can do, and then—"

Ernesto stepped forward, pulling on the sleeves of his prized white leather jacket. "Hey, Mrs. Dunne! I'm the message guy. Remember?" And then he leaned closer to David and whispered, "It's not really my territory, though, so can you help me out on this one?"

"Sure, Ernesto," David whispered. "It's as good as done."

David turned to Natalie, noticing for the first time the new hue of her spiked tresses. Pink. "Hey, Natalie, going for the feminine look?"

"Right, pinhead," she said, smiling. "See ya in fifty or sixty."

Jason nervously shifted his feet. "Are you sure about this, bro?"

David hated to leave his best friend behind, but he knew that the way time was all out of whack up here, it probably wouldn't seem like much more than a blink before he was back. "Yeah, I'm sure," he said. "I've got a few loose ends to tie up. I might even try out for the West City League again. Maybe they need a batboy. But listen, Jason, if they offer you a guardian-angel job—take it—you can come and be mine. We could really pull some good ones on Mrs. Graves."

Jason smiled and nodded. He reached out to shake David's hand one last time, but then threw his arms around him instead. David hugged his best friend, unashamed. "You better get going," Jason finally said, pushing away as he swiped at the corner of his eye.

"Later," they both said.

David turned and walked away, but then called out over his shoulder, "And, Mrs. Dunne, if they offer you any jobs, make sure they don't involve sharp right turns!" He waved and hurried back to the Waiting Room.

12
New Spots

THE WAITING ROOM door seemed so far away. Soon—
very soon he would be back in his old body. Back in
his old life. But it wouldn't be his old life—exactly. It
would be different. Hopefully not slimy different, or
arms-falling-off-in-the-aisle different. But different in
ways that were important. A leopard's spots may not
change overnight, but David felt certain that his had
already taken on a slightly different hue. He would
go back in just minutes. Marie would probably—

David froze. His temples pounded. *Marie! Jeez!*
He had forgotten to even mention her when he was
talking to God! Or did he? Did he say she had to
go back, too? Did he say she was part of the deal?
He couldn't remember. Damn! What *did* he say? He

wouldn't go back without her, no matter what. He wouldn't forget his promise! *Never!*

The Waiting Room doorknob burned in his hands as he threw open the door. "Marie!" he yelled, but the floor was not there and he felt himself falling...falling. Soft, warm air gently rippled across his cheeks as he continued to fall...to return. He was surprised. He wasn't frightened. It felt as natural going back to his life as death must have seemed to Jason. The time was right. He could hear a quiet hush race past his ears, like an evening desert wind. He savored this neverland halfway between death and life, knowing it was a whisper of time that he might one day believe was just a dream.

The speck that had slipped from his grasp now loomed into view. Though he knew a vanload of passengers sprinkled the ground below him, the only speck—the only life—he could see was his own. He focused in on the growing speck, like a ship on a beacon of light. Home. The speck took on form. Arms. Legs. His own lifeless face. But still he was not frightened. His muscles were relaxed, light, as he prepared to take back what was his. He hovered now, not like the police helicopter at his death, but like a seagull riding the air currents. He felt a final *whoosh,* and he was back.

13

Ⓞuch

OH, MAN! The words didn't come from his lips, but reverberated throughout his head like a clanging cymbal. It was too painful to move his lips, tongue, anything. His arms, his legs, everything was so heavy. He felt like he was being pressed down into the dirt and gravel below him. He couldn't breathe, and yet he had to. He forced the air into his lungs, but the rising of his chest sent convulsing waves of pain around to his back. *Give up! Give up!* But he wouldn't give up—ever! He pushed the air back out of his lungs, sending the searing pain back around to his chest. A writhing groan escaped from his mouth as he forced his lungs to repeat the whole gruesome process.

"Hey! We've got a live one over here!"

Words, voices, drifted into his consciousness. He couldn't tell where they were coming from. Maybe his own head. *Breathe.*

"Bring down a board! I need some help here!"

David forced his eyelids open, certain that the effort was splitting his skull in two. His eyes wouldn't focus, but he could see blurred images moving past his feet. Paramedics? Was someone here to help him? *Just take a rock and crush my skull. Finish the job and put me out of my misery. No. No! Breathe, you butthead. Breathe. Help me.*

He felt a tug on his arm and then a prick. He was alive. *Alive.* He wouldn't give up. The images became more focused. *Blue. Yellow.* He could see badges, straps, an oxygen mask being lowered to his face. More voices.

"My God! This kid with the dreadlocks lost his insides all over this other kid! What should I do with this stuff?"

"Just scoop it off. He won't be needing it anymore."

"Booger!" David groaned, irritated that Booger had once again "spilled" on him. *But at least they aren't my own guts,* he thought. One problem solved.

"Dead female over here. Approximately sixteen."

No! She's not dead! Give her a chance! Marie! David groaned and tried to turn his head in the direction of the voice.

"Purple hair. No I.D."

Natalie! It's not, Marie. At least not yet. He heard the voice identify the others one by one: Dead female, approximately fifty. Dead Hispanic male, black-leather jacket. Dead white male, letterman's jacket. He heard sirens and tape ripping from its roll as every inch of his body was immobilized. He tried to hear beyond the ripping sound, to the muffled voices. He had to know. Were there more?

"Son? Can you hear me?"

A face loomed over his. It wasn't his dad. *Why is he calling me "son"?* The face sharpened into focus, then faded out again.

"What's your name, son? Do you know your name?"

Who is this clown? Of course I know my name. Where is Marie? That was all he cared about. "Marie," he moaned.

"He thinks his name's Marie. His license says David James. What about the day, son? What day is today?"

What difference does it make? But David figured this guy wouldn't go away until he answered his lame questions. Let's see, he had been in heaven for at least a day, so it must be Friday. "Friday," he rasped.

"It's Thursday, David. Thursday. One-forty in the afternoon. Remember? You were on a field trip."

One-forty! That's impossible, David thought. He had only been gone five minutes! Was it all just a dream? A horrible psychotic dream?

"Okay, son. This might be a little bumpy, but we'll make it as smooth a ride as we can. We're gonna carry you up the hill to the ambulance now. Hang on."

If it wouldn't have hurt so much, David would have snockered out a laugh to rival Tom Hanks's. Hang on? He was plastered to the body board with six miles of silver tape! He didn't need to hang on to anything! His eyes were becoming more focused now, and he could see two uniformed men at the foot of the board, carrying him up the hillside. He groaned in pain with each bump, each jostle, though the groaning itself only added to his pain. *Jeez!* He could be at a concert right now with Jason...maybe that was where Marie was... or was she part of a dream, too?

"Just a little farther now, David. We're almost there. That IV is going to help with your pain. Don't you worry now." They reached the top of the hillside and stepped through the twisted wreckage of the broken guardrail. They laid him on a waiting gurney just outside of the ambulance and talked some more on their scratchy phones.

"Sam!" David called. "Tell me! Where is she?"

David couldn't turn his head, but suddenly something on the floor of the ambulance caught his eye. He strained his eyes to the right to see what it was. Pink... something pink. He strained until his head turned slightly, even under the restraint of the tape. Pink... rose petals. It was pink rose petals!

"Marie!" he yelled. "Marie!"

He heard his cry returned with a very weak, almost inaudible, "David."

"Hey, son! Calm down. Is that your friend's name? We'll get you in there to see her in just a second." David felt another prick in his arm and then the gurney was pushed into the right side of the ambulance.

"So what took you so long?" she asked. "Goofin' off somewhere?" Her voice was weak, broken, with ragged breaths between words, but it was Marie's. *Marie.* She had made it back. They had won. He had kept his promise to her.

"Sorry," David groaned, "I didn't mean to keep Her Royal Dweebness waiting."

"A red one, David," Marie whispered.

The words were sapping his strength, but he had to know what she was blathering about now. "More information, Marie," he whispered back.

"My corsage. For the prom"—she grimaced—"I want it to be red."

David smiled, even though every muscle in his face protested in pain. "No problem," he said. "No problem at all."